CENTURION

CENTURION

A Novel of Ancient Rome

Peter W. Mitsopoulos

Copyright © 2001 by Peter W. Mitsopoulos.

Library of Congress Number:		2001118414
ISBN #:	Hardcover	1-4010-2741-5
	Softcover	1-4010-2740-7

All rights reserved. No part of this book may be reproduced or transmitted in any form or by any means, electronic or mechanical, including photocopying, recording, or by any information storage and retrieval system, without permission in writing from the copyright owner.

This is a work of fiction. Names, characters, places and incidents either are the product of the author's imagination or are used fictitiously, and any resemblance to any actual persons, living or dead, events, or locales is entirely coincidental.

Cover illustration by Joanna R. Bonomi.

This book was printed in the United States of America.

To order additional copies of this book, contact:
Xlibris Corporation
1-888-7-XLIBRIS
www.Xlibris.com
Orders@Xlibris.com

For my parents, Anna and William,
and for my sister, Genevieve

I

"Tortoise!" bellowed Glaxus. "Now!"

The ambush was swift, but his century's response matched it. The sound of shields clanking together overhead and on all sides was instantaneous. He had long drilled his troops on the need for obedience and coolness under pressure. At times, he had literally beaten it into them. Now it was saving their lives yet again and confounding the Gauls. Only howls of disappointment penetrated the formation as stones and arrows were repelled. Even so, Glaxus knew standing still for too long would be disastrous.

In his place at the formation's front, he moved his shield aside slightly to get a look forward. Six of his men who were scouting ahead had been caught beyond the tortoise's reach and were now fighting for their lives. Finding the tortoise a waste of weapons and energy, most of the Gauls were hurling themselves at this unlucky group. They clearly wanted to kill at least a few Romans before returning to the cover of the woods. Outnumbered four or five to one, the scouts had cleverly bought themselves time by forming a circle, their backs to its center.

On his right, he heard Macro hissing through clenched teeth. "By all the gods, Glaxus! We must reach them!"

"Silence! I can see as well as you!" He tightened his grip on his javelin. "Porcupine forward at standard pace! Now!"

The formation suddenly sprouted spearheads, instantly impaling three Gaulish warriors. At the same moment it began a slow, smooth advance. One of the embattled half-dozen now glanced directly into Glaxus' eyes. He was young Arminius, in the army barely three months and already seeing his first action.

The Gauls surrounding the scouts saw the porcupine coming. Glaxus wondered if they would try a suicide attack, dozens of them throwing themselves onto the Roman spears. This could drag the formation apart, forcing the century to fight the barbarians man to man. He decided he wouldn't give them time to consider it.

"Double-pace!"

The formation surged forward. Just as it reached the six, Glaxus saw one of them cleanly beheaded by a naked Gaul wearing gold armbands. A chieftain by his body paint, he quickly tried to reach down for his trophy. Glaxus had seen Roman heads hung from trees as a means of Gaulish intimidation.

"Not today!" he shouted, and rammed his javelin at the chieftain.

The Gaul was bent over with his back to the porcupine and so took the iron spearhead directly between his buttocks. Wailing in agony, he tried to stand and pull away, but it was too late.

"Like a pig on a spit!" snarled Macro.

The chieftain dropped heavily into the damp grass as the javelin snapped off in Glaxus' hand. It was indeed a miserable way for a proud warrior to die, but Glaxus learned long ago that opportunities in combat had to be seized. He threw down the broken shaft and drew his sword.

Leaderless and facing resolute resistance, the Gauls began disappearing into the foggy woods, dragging along their injured. Glaxus took immediate advantage of this. "Open, Macro!" He and Macro slid their shields apart and the five survivors slipped into the formation.

Glaxus glanced over his shoulder. "Wounds?" he barked.

Arminius spoke for the others. "Nothing serious, Centurion. Some broken fingers, a toe chopped off. We'll be all right until we reach the fort."

"Number of enemy killed and wounded by your group?"

"Three killed. Several more badly wounded and may die later."

Glaxus saw a chance to mete out reward and knew better than to let it pass. Such opportunities were more useful in the legions than those for meting out punishment.

"Standard marching formation," he ordered. When this was done, he stepped to the head of the column and called forward the five surviving scouts.

"Which of you thought to form the circle when you were blocked from reaching the tortoise?"

Four of them looked at the fifth, at Arminius.

"Was it you, soldier?"

"Yes sir."

"Well done. You saved the lives of most of your fellow scouts." Glaxus reached down and pulled the two gold bands from the arms of the dead chieftain. They were rare prizes to which he could claim a right, having been the one to kill the Gaul. Then again, selfishness in a leader earned no loyalty. He handed both bands to Arminius.

"You will melt one down and distribute its gold evenly to these four. The second you will keep entirely for yourself. I shall also mention your quick thinking to the Chief Centurion." Glaxus decided Arminius would bear watching and possibly rapid promotion.

"Will we take our fallen comrade back to the fort for cremation?" asked Macro.

"Yes, but first lop the head off this painted dog and string it from a tree." Glaxus prodded the chieftain's body with his foot. "Let the Gauls see one of theirs dangle in the wind for a change."

Macro whipped out his sword. "Yes sir!"

To Glaxus' relief, the hour-long march to the fort was uneventful. Leaving the century at their barracks, he accompanied the wounded to the physician. As Pindocles began treatment, Glaxus stayed to watch. Arminius grimaced when his fingers were probed for breaks. Pindocles appeared to take no notice and kept squeezing the young man's knuckles.

Glaxus believed some encouragement was in order. "My troops are tough," he said with a grin. "A little pain only makes them tougher."

While Arminius and the others laughed, Pindocles spoke softly to Glaxus. "Upon returning from patrol, is it not mandatory to report to the Chief Centurion?"

Having been transferred to Germanic Gaul nearly a year ago, Glaxus had no serious complaints about anyone he served with here, including Pindocles. Still, he was always uncomfortable around this Greek. The man's words often had a ring of arrogance.

Glaxus tried to reply in an even voice. "Plutarius will be informed of our return and knows I will report to him shortly. If I didn't see to my men first, he would be angry."

"The esteemed Plutarius also knows I am a master of the healing arts and that your men are in good hands."

"Are they? One of them returned with his head in a sack. Can you heal that, you Greek braggart?" Glaxus turned his back on Pindocles and walked out of the infirmary. Behind him, he could practically hear the physician smiling.

A detail of troops was putting new tiles on the roof of the headquarters building. "About time," muttered Glaxus. The place had been leaking like a sieve for days. Inside he found Macro standing with Plutarius, who waved him over.

"Come in, Glaxus. Your optio has been telling me of the ambush. Your century acquitted itself well, as usual."

"Thank you, sir. But although we were attacked, I can report that we saw no signs of the tribes massing for an assault on the fort. The alliance would seem to be holding. Our attackers were likely a pack of raiders from a non-allied tribe."

"Bah!" snorted Macro. "These Germanics never seem to know whose side they're on. They form alliances with each other, or with us, and then break them on a whim. We need to cross the Rhine again and establish settlers in that territory one way or another. General Drusus began it twenty years ago and we should finish it."

Plutarius nudged an elbow into Macro's side. "It's as though you see into the future, my friend, though we may be able to use more peaceful means than Drusus did."

"How so?" asked Glaxus? "Is something afoot?" He'd heard rumors, but army life was riddled with those, most proving to be false.

"Yes," said Plutarius. "Couriers from Rome arrived an hour ago with dispatches bearing the imperial seal."

Glaxus was impressed. Dispatches directly from Emperor Augustus didn't come along every day. This most likely meant the eastern Gauls had agreed to permit a major colonization campaign. But who would command? Perhaps Tiberius was returning to Germania after being sent to deal with the uprising in Pannonia. Or would it be some patrician from Rome who didn't know one end of a sword from the other?

The Chief Centurion pointed to a closed door at the far end of the hallway. "The Legate has been studying the orders since they were delivered. When he's ready, he'll inform the tribunes and I of their content. We'll then call a meeting of centurions and pass on the information."

Macro looked toward the door. "I wish I could go into the council room with you, sir," he told Plutarius. "I'd like to hear it straight from the Legate himself."

"Wish in one pail and piss in another," said Glaxus. "See which fills up first. We must accept things as they are, Macro. Duty and discipline are our lot."

Plutarius clapped his hands on their shoulders. "True enough, comrades. And since advancement comes to those who do the difficult, let us pray to the gods our new orders are nearly impossible, for the greater the reward if we succeed." He tapped Macro on the helmet. "Besides, you're a good optio. Glaxus tells me so regularly. You should be a centurion in time, then perhaps a senior centurion. Someday you could even have my job. Then you can attend war council."

"Perhaps," grunted Macro. "If one of these barbarians doesn't hack my balls off first."

Plutarius laughed. "In which case, you can return to Rome and be a eunuch servant to the Emperor's wife." He eased Macro toward the exit. "It's been a long day and the time has come for food and rest. Glaxus, stay a moment. I must speak with you."

When Macro was gone, Plutarius lowered his voice. "Your optio tells me one of your soldiers distinguished himself today and was handsomely compensated."

"Yes sir. I was going to mention him to you myself. His name is Arminius. He was courageous and quick-witted and I thought it best not to let him go unnoticed or unrewarded."

"At the cost to yourself of two gold armbands? It was you who killed the Gaul."

"It was also I who got one soldier beheaded by letting the scouts stray too far from the formation."

"Scouts can't scout if they're not some distance forward. It's risky duty, but we've all taken our turn at it."

"Yes sir, but I just didn't feel right claiming the gold. Arminius and the other four can have it."

Plutarius stroked his graying beard. "Credit and blame where they are due. A Roman invention which you use well, my friend, even with yourself. Perhaps that accounts for your steady rise over the years." He put a hand on Glaxus' arm. "Yet you would do well to watch Arminius closely."

"I plan to, sir. If he continues to perform with distinction, I'll recommend him for promotion."

"Yes, yes, that's all well and good. But another reason to keep an eye on him is that he's a Germanic Gaul."

"In the regular Roman army?" Glaxus couldn't believe it. "Gauls can only serve in our auxiliary forces."

"He's a special member of the Cherusci tribe, so an exception was made. In his own tongue he's called Herman."

Glaxus had certainly heard of the Cherusci. They recently became Rome's principal ally against the lesser Germanic tribes. As

Macro had said, such alliances rarely lasted, yet the Emperor kept trying.

"And what makes this Herman so special, sir?"

"He's the favorite son-in-law of Segestes."

Glaxus suddenly understood. Segestes was chief of chiefs among the Cherusci. He once came to the fort for a meeting with the Legate to discuss terms of the alliance and the forming of Gaulish auxiliary units. Glaxus and Plutarius had met him at the gates. The tribal leader's head and face were covered with blonde hair and he was no less than a javelin-length in height. Surprised to find Glaxus didn't need to look up at him, he said he hadn't thought a Roman pig could grow so tall. Glaxus replied he never thought a six-foot Gaulish snake could stand on its tail. The chieftain and his men had laughed and called this a fair response.

Those events were some three months ago, Glaxus recalled, shortly before Arminius joined his century. He'd assumed the new blue-eyed soldier was from northern Italia. He didn't ask his men idle questions about their families or backgrounds, preferring to keep his relationship with them professional and rooted in the present.

"Has Augustus made Segestes and Arminius Roman citizens in return for the alliance?"

"Only Segestes for now," said Plutarius. "But Augustus allowed Arminius to join the army despite being a non-citizen and married. After proving himself in the regular army, he'll be granted citizenship and given command of a Gaulish auxiliary unit. The Emperor so favors them as a reward for their loyalty."

Glaxus didn't think highly of this arrangement. It wasn't fair. "Citizenship before being allowed to enlist is what keeps the Roman army Roman, sir. And staying formally single throughout the twenty-year enlistment is something every legionary lives with. Exceptions are not appreciated by the rest of us."

"Which is why you will keep it to yourself, Centurion. Clear?"

Glaxus knew only one answer was possible. "Yes sir."

The Chief Centurion studied his subordinate briefly before smiling. "Besides, can we argue with the Emperor?"

"Of course not." Glaxus hesitated a moment, then added, "May I ask how long you have known this, sir?"

"The Legate was told by the Emperor himself before leaving Rome. He told me upon his arrival and ordered me to assign Arminius to one of the five senior centurions. I was to tell you at a time I considered appropriate, and I've done so. If Arminius is distinguishing himself and you are considering him for promotion, then the time has come for you to know."

"Shall I tell him I do?"

"No. Keep him guessing and treat him as you treat the others. Just be sure you watch him like an owl."

"Yes sir. Like an owl."

"Now get some rest, Glaxus. We'll speak again later."

Out on the assembly ground, Glaxus slowly untied his helmet strap and headed for his barracks. So there was a Gaulish tribesman in his century. Who said the gods had no sense of humor? But son-in-law of a chieftain or not, Arminius would be treated exactly as Plutarius wanted, no differently from the other soldiers. If he fell in battle, as he nearly did today, then so be it. There would be nothing to do but stand back and let the horse dung hit the wind.

As Glaxus neared his barracks, he looked at the guards on the parapet over the main gate. One of them, no older than eighteen, was leaning against the stone wall.

"You don't need to hold the fort up, soldier!"

The startled guard leaped away from the wall and stood at attention. "Yes sir!" From the markings on his javelin he was a member of Quintar's century.

"Your comrades are depending on you to be alert!"

"Yes sir!"

Glaxus remembered his own cockiness at that age and knew the best cure for it. "Your centurion has surely told you of the penalty for falling asleep on guard duty."

The dread on the soldier's young face was unmistakable. "Yes sir! But I won't, sir!"

"We will see."

After passing a hard stare over all the guards for good measure, Glaxus entered the quarters he shared with Macro at the west end of the barracks. While getting Macro to help him off with his ring mail, he decided to make a walk-through.

"What is the century doing? They had better be resting."

"I so ordered," said Macro. "Also, Arminius and the other four returned from the infirmary and requested permission to melt down one of the gold bands."

"You granted this permission?" asked Glaxus coldly.

"Uh, yes sir. I thought since they bore the brunt of things today, they . . . they . . ."

"They might be allowed to have their reward immediately?"

Macro became a little flustered. "Well, yes sir. I—"

"Well done," snapped Glaxus. "A good command decision." He watched Macro smile. Even one's optio had to be tested now and then. No one knew this better than Macro. "Where are those five?"

"Outside the door at the far end."

Walking slowly and deliberately through the barracks hall, Glaxus made sure the hobnails on his sandals clicked loudly on the wooden floor. Most of his men were stretched on their cots, some asleep, some scrawling letters on pieces of birch sapwood. They surely would have preferred wax-coated wooden tablets, but those were difficult to obtain at a distant outpost. Only Pindocles had a steady supply. One of the Legate's own slaves made them especially for him. Glaxus sneered at the thought. Birchbark wasn't good enough for the great healing master.

Two soldiers were sitting on their bunks, a game of robbers placed on a stool between them. They nervously glanced up from the board as Glaxus passed.

"One match only, then sleep."

"Yes, Centurion."

Reaching the open door at the opposite end of the barracks, Glaxus saw Arminius and his four friends about ten paces from the building. They were gathered around a fire above which they had hung a small cauldron. Arminius dropped in a gold band as the others bent over to watch.

"Look how quickly it melts," said one.

"That's because it's pure gold," explained Arminius. "Mixing it with a another metal would make it more durable, but the chieftains like it pure. They say it better befits their rank."

"How do you know that?" joked another. "Been out drinking with the Gauls, have you?"

The rest laughed, but Arminius only smiled faintly. When he slipped the second band into the cauldron with the first, Glaxus was surprised and stepped forward.

"Centurion!" exclaimed one of the five, and they all straightened up.

"At ease," ordered Glaxus. He observed the glittering yellow liquid in the cauldron, then turned to Arminius. "You have melted them both together. Did I not say you had to melt and distribute only one and that you could keep the other?"

"Yes sir, you did, but I decided it wasn't fair to keep so much for myself. My comrades faced just as much danger today, so I thought it better to melt down both and distribute the gold into six equal portions."

"Six? There are only five of you."

Arminius glanced at the others, who were obviously expecting him to do the talking.

"Sir, I plan to send the sixth portion to the family of our dead comrade. We all agreed it was the right thing to do."

"This was your idea, soldier?"

"Yes sir."

Glaxus was impressed. Such thinking in a legionary of the lowest rank was unusual, but then Arminius was an unusual legionary. "You know the mail is often unreliable. Even when it works, it takes months to get letters and packets from one part of the empire to another. His name was Drinian, but I don't know his hometown."

Arminius did. "Herculaneum, sir, south of Rome. He told me once his parents were not wealthy."

"Then let us hope the gods will guide it safely there. Now, finish up and get into your cots. The sun is almost set."

Perhaps the Emperor knew what he was doing by promising an eventual auxiliary command to Arminius. As Glaxus returned through the barracks, he had to admit this Gaul seemed more astute than many of the superstitious young Romans in the army. A natural leader as well, judging from how the others deferred to him. That was fortunate, because superior ability would soon get Arminius his superior position, then he would no longer be Glaxus' problem.

At next day's dawn, all fifty-four of the legion's centurions were instructed to assemble in front of headquarters. Tridonis Varunus stood on the command platform, his legate's helmet shining in the rising sun. To his right was Plutarius, absolutely motionless. Behind Tridonis, his six tribunes stood in a more relaxed manner, occasionally putting their heads together in pairs to exchange whispers. They were all young patricians using army service to boost their careers when they returned to Rome. Because of their privileged birth, they could serve much less than twenty years. To Glaxus, they were primping peacocks who cared only about wine, women, and personal advancement.

Glaxus next studied Tridonis, who was waiting patiently for the centurions to take their places. The scar on his cheekbone showed darkly above his bristling beard. Not many legates bore the marks of battle, but then Tridonis was nothing like others of his rank. He was the first man in more than a hundred years to rise from common soldier to command a legion, being personally chosen for it by the Emperor. This was why the troops adored him and the tribunes resented him.

When everyone was in place, Plutarius called for silence before stepping back. The Legate's high voice then cut through the cool air. "I have received orders from his Imperial Majesty. The alliance is secured. The territory northeast of the Rhine will therefore be colonized. Two more legions accompanied by settlers are en route from Rome under the supreme command of General Quintilius Varus. This legion will also be placed under his leadership."

Tridonis paused to sweep his eyes over his centurions. "You are the backbone of the legions. Without you, there would be no army. Without the army, there would be no Rome. Without Rome, the world would have no form or shape. You are the instrument by which the gods bring order out of chaos. Whether the alliance holds or not, the colonies will be established." The Legate clutched his sword handle. "Failure is inconceivable."

Tridonis gestured toward Plutarius, then descended from the platform with the tribunes trailing behind. As they disappeared into the headquarters building, the Chief Centurion spoke.

"The legions that join us are the 17th and 18th. They left Rome sixty days ago and the main column should arrive within the week. Mounted scouts riding ahead could be here tomorrow or even today. We will send out a group of our own cavalry scouts to meet them. There will undoubtedly be mail and packets for everyone. Return to your troops and pass on what you have been told." Plutarius struck his right fist over his heart, then extended that arm in salute. "Hail the Emperor."

Glaxus walked back to the barracks area with Quintar.

"The Emperor be damned! That old swillbag Augustus doesn't have to shed his blood or see a friend's head hang from a branch."

"You speak thus of our noble leader?" laughed Glaxus. "The grand-nephew and adopted heir of the great Julius Caesar?"

Quintar scowled. "Heir, but not equal. Caesar has been dead for fifty-three years. Rome hasn't seen his like since and never will."

"But he didn't attempt conquests northeast of the Rhine," countered Glaxus. "Subduing the rest of Gaul was enough, even for his pride."

"Perhaps it should be so for us, as well. Perhaps Rome reaches too far, Glaxus, and assumes too much. What do you think?"

Glaxus was inclined to scoff at this question. How could the views of a lone centurion matter? Then he noticed his comrade's serious face and restrained himself. "The Emperor commands, we obey. What else can I think, Quintar?"

"Can you imagine the world without Rome?"

"You heard the Legate. Without Rome, there is no world. But let the sages and scholars wrestle with all that. You and I are soldiers and should attend to our duty. Speaking of which, I saw one of your men leaning against a wall while on guard yesterday."

Glaxus saw the fire suddenly rekindle in Quintar's eyes.

"I'll flay the hide off his lazy bones! Who was it?"

"A smooth faced young dolt. Fresh off the farm, from the look of him."

"Arius, no doubt. He should still be at his mother's tits, not facing Gaulish warriors."

"The vinestick across his back once or twice should do it." Glaxus turned off toward his barracks. "But no more than that."

"Once only," promised Quintar as they parted.

Glaxus kicked at a clod of mud and considered his friend's remarks. Did Rome truly overreach? He frowned and tried to push the idea away.

Arriving at the barracks, he saw Arminius and three other soldiers approaching with shovels, their legs and arms covered with thick muck. They stood at attention when they saw him.

"You were performing some task?"

"Yes sir," Arminius answered. "The Optio had us excavate fresh sanitation holes in the woods on the hill."

Glaxus wondered briefly how the Emperor would like it if he knew one of his favorites was digging a shit pit. "The hill on the east side of the fort overlooking headquarters? Then you could hear the Legate speak of our new orders."

"Yes sir," said Arminius. "His voice carried up to us easily."

Quintar's words of a moment ago were still with Glaxus and he decided to try something. "What did you think?"

Of the four, only Arminius didn't appear stunned. "Our thoughts count for nothing, Centurion," he replied. "The Emperor requires obedience, not opinions."

Glaxus knew he had to be satisfied with this answer. Hadn't he said the same thing to Quintar? What else could a Roman soldier of any rank say? He was about to order them to get cleaned up when Arminius spoke again.

"I just hope, sir, that General Varus considers his actions carefully."

How was that remark to be taken? "I'm sure a Roman General always does so," said Glaxus. "Now, rinse yourselves off and get into your armor. I will assemble the century presently."

Glaxus found Macro sitting on his cot, shining his ring mail and bronze helmet. "I want them polished up to look my best when General Varus arrives."

"Why?"

"I must do what it takes to impress my superiors. I've been in ten years now and I'm still not a centurion."

Glaxus sat on his cot across from Macro. "Took me eleven, you know. And another four after that to make senior centurion. Most serve their entire twenty and never make it above optio."

"I must, and soon. Being a centurion will give me a better chance when I apply to the Praetorian Guard."

"You want to be one of the Emperor's personal troops? The odds against that are long indeed."

"I still plan to try." Macro looked up from his gleaming helmet. "Why don't you apply, Glaxus? You're more than two yards high, built like a brick wall, and you were born in Rome. You're just what the Guard prefers. Combine that with your decorations for valor in combat and they'd accept you instantly."

"So I can strut the streets of Rome like a pompous jackass? No, thank you. I'll finish my career in the regular army."

"As you wish, but getting to Rome a year sooner would provide you with a certain opportunity, wouldn't it?"

Now Macro was getting too familiar. "Polish your armor, Optio. The century will assemble soon and a professional attitude will be expected from all." Glaxus stood and opened the armory door. "Plain enough?"

"Yes sir." But then Macro added, "She may have realized her mistake by now and changed her mind."

"Who said she made a mistake?" growled Glaxus, and strode into the armory to select a javelin.

Thirty minutes later, centuries were noisily forming up across the assembly ground. A thick fog had fallen over the fort. This was common year-round in the Germanic forests, though that fact didn't stop Glaxus' men from saying it was a bad omen, coming just as they received new orders. In his usual style, Macro was walking around the formation telling the complainers to shut up or forfeit their teeth. Off to the left, Glaxus heard Quintar shouting similar things to his century.

After nineteen years in the army, Glaxus had trouble believing in omens. If you were tougher and better trained than your adversary, as the Roman army usually was, you'd likely win. If not, you could expect to lose. And weren't omens a matter of perspective? A bad one for your side was a good one for the enemy. Glaxus considered it better to be done with them and trust entirely in planning and preparation.

When his troops were quiet and Macro had brought them to attention, Glaxus quickly related what he'd heard at the meeting of centurions.

"And that's all I can tell you for now," he concluded. "We'll obviously know more details about the campaign when General Varus arrives with his legions. They will also bring mail, as well as the latest news from Rome and the rest of the empire. As soon as the mail is received and sorted, it will be distributed. In the meantime, today is our day for drilling with sword and javelin." Glaxus pointed at Macro. "The Optio will lead you while I observe. Our assigned drilling ground is outside the main gate on the right."

After marching through the gate, the century took their positions and Glaxus reminded them of the basics once again. He knew he couldn't say it too often.

"When fighting on open ground, one battle formation against another, you must advance in a uniform line and wait until your enemy is within proper striking range before throwing. Too far and your javelins fall short, too close and there's not enough force behind them. You can only carry two and both must be made to count. A direct hit on your enemy's shield is what you want."

Glaxus examined his javelin to be sure the two-foot soft iron shaft was firmly attached to the four-foot wooden handle. He then aimed at a target shield mounted on a post and made his throw. The javelin's point imbedded itself in the shield's upper half. The soft shaft immediately bent under the weight of the handle until the handle's end touched the ground.

"Your enemy will have trouble using his shield or walking forward because the handle catches in the ground. If he tries to pull out your first javelin, he must reach around his shield to do so. You then throw your second javelin into his exposed body. If he tries to continue advancing without pulling it out, put your second javelin into his shield with the first. His shield will now be too heavy and he must drop it. He is then vulnerable to our archers, or from behind your own shield you may use your blade and safely stab him full of holes."

Glaxus drew his sword. "Stand too close together and you will disembowel each other instead of your enemy. A yard and a half apart is about right. Stay behind your shield and always thrust, never slash. Slashing leaves you open to a counterstroke. A thrust is also harder to block, especially after your opponent has been deshielded." Glaxus demonstrated, jabbing the weapon forward with a quick twisting motion. "Attack his belly. Enough practice, and you'll have him stepping in his own guts before he knows it. And keep a firm grip on your sword because your dagger is only an emergency weapon."

He glared at his men. "And remember to stay calm always and depend on your comrades to do their duty as skillfully as you do yours, even in conditions other than a pitched battle. If we must fight the Gauls among the trees in disorderly brawls, we will. Roman courage and discipline worked for us in yesterday's ambush and will do so again." He nodded at Macro. "Take them through it. Javelins first."

It was in the middle of javelin drill that the fort's mounted scouts returned, riding past with advance scouts from the approaching legions. Just after midday, during the first round of sword drills, the mail wagons rolled through the gate accompanied by a cavalry escort. When Glaxus hailed him, one of the horse soldiers said General Varus and the main column would probably arrive tomorrow afternoon, earlier than first thought.

An hour before sunset, messengers came from Plutarius telling all centurions that mail had been sorted by century and delivered to each barracks. Permission was immediately granted to end drills and work details so as to begin the evening meal early. The distribution of mail could then commence. Upon bringing his century from the cookhouse to the barracks, Glaxus ordered everyone to sit on their cots. He opened one of the two woolen sacks to grab a handful of wooden tablets and began calling names. The men quickly passed each tablet along to its recipient, laughing and making jokes if they thought it was from a sweetheart.

"Does she miss you, Serbius? That's what they always write!"

"But they practice with someone else's javelin while you're gone!"

"You should have had her once more before you left! I did!"

Besides the tablets, there were leather packets containing money, good luck charms, dried fruit, and small jugs of olive oil. Glaxus emptied the sacks without finding anything for Macro or himself. Now that both his parents were dead, he expected no mail, but nothing for his optio was surprising. Macro normally got several letters and packets from various relatives. Arminius meanwhile was accepting a dried fig from a comrade while listening attentively as another read a letter aloud. As always, he hadn't received mail either. The reason was no longer a mystery.

Stepping out of the barracks hall into his quarters, Glaxus saw half a dozen tablets and packets on Macro's cot. There was a solitary tablet on his. Before he could touch it, Macro came in behind him.

"I slipped away from the cookhouse ahead of the century and got our mail out of the bags first. I hope you don't mind."

Glaxus threw his cloak on and picked up the tablet. "I don't mind," he said, and went outside to read it by torchlight.

The night air was cool and a half-moon was hanging over the tips of the pine trees just outside the fort's east wall. Glaxus stood under one of the torches placed around the assembly ground. He had recognized the handwriting as soon as he saw his name on the tablet's exterior.

>Glaxus Claudius Valtinius, Senior Centurion
>19th Legion—4th Cohort—Lead Century
>Fort Vetera, Lower Germania

Nearly a year after he left, he had received a letter from Calvinia.

II

2nd of July,
762 From the City's Founding

Glaxus,

You must think it strange for me to write you after the way we parted and after so much time has passed. Please read on. There is much I could not tell you then which I am free to relate now.

The first thing you must know is that I have broken the betrothal I told you about. Also, my father died of a fever not long after being expelled from the senate for taking bribes. As further punishment, he was required by Emperor Augustus to surrender his personal fortune. After the expulsion, I felt I would have to accept a proposal from Senator Marcus Hyboreas. With his great wealth he could have restored my father's estate.

There was certainly no affection involved. I would have been his fifth wife. He was merely seeking one more trophy and would have tossed me aside with the others soon enough. Divorce has become so common in Rome that it would appall our ancestors. Perhaps such is the price we pay for prosperity and self-indulgence. I am looked upon as odd for not remarrying two or three time since my husband's death.

Hyboreas was willing to marry the impoverished and widowed daughter of a disgraced senator, but only if I kept my mouth shut and my legs apart. Father said I had to endure such a marriage for only a year and then the divorce payment would enrich us again. But by the mercy of the gods his scheming and shame ended with his life, as did the need to prostitute myself. I'm relieved my mother didn't live to see any of this.

You left Rome knowing only that I refused your proposal while accepting another. You must have thought me a conceited flirt who had only been playing with your feelings.

I wish I could have told you of these things at the time, but father begged me not to. He had foreseen his expulsion from the senate and was already making plans to match me with Hyboreas. As you well know, he didn't believe there was any advantage in my marrying a plebeian soldier. I'll never forget the day he told you so to your face. I'm very sorry for that.

Shortly after you left for Germania, the expulsion took place and became public knowledge. I didn't write to you sooner because I was so mortified at how you had been treated. I was sure you wanted nothing more to do with me. Following my father's death, I borrowed a small sum of money from his sister with which to become a butcher in the Emporium district of the city. I live in a room above my shop.

The people here don't know I'm the daughter of a senator. As you can imagine, I don't want that to change. I've had quite a transition from spinning fine linen in my father's mansion to being elbow-deep in pig's blood. I can see why patricians such as myself are taught to look down our noses at plebeians and slaves. Otherwise we might discover whose labor supports our luxury. I always assumed the roast pork would just appear on my father's table. I never cared to know how it got there or who made it possible. I know now.

And thus things are, Glaxus. As for the future, who can say? By the time these words reach you, if they reach you at all, you should have only a month or two left in your enlistment. Will you return to Rome upon your discharge?

There is word on the streets that Quintilius Varus leads a great force to join your legion for a major campaign in Germania. I met him once at a dinner party given by my father. He's arrogant and corrupt, vices he readily developed as one of Rome's consuls twenty-two years ago and after that as governor of Syria. He's a lawyer with no military ability, but has long been a friend and favorite of Augustus, probably because of his marriage to the Emperor's niece. Connections seem to matter more than skill these days. I know how important your duty is to you, but be as careful as you can under his command.

My shop and my home, such as they be, lie at the west end of Via Mercurius in the Emporium, in the 18th precinct of the 13th ward. I'm sure I'll be there for a while to come.

May the gods guide and protect you.

—Calvinia

Glaxus felt as though a blindfold had been removed from his eyes. He closed the tablet and hid it under his cloak. A detachment carrying return mail would be headed to Rome not long after Varus' arrival. This in mind, he immediately looked toward the infirmary and was glad to see an oil lamp glowing in one of its windows.

Striding swiftly across the assembly ground, he stepped through the open door. Inside, he found the lamp hanging over a table on which lay the headless body of Drinian. Pindocles was bent over it with a scalpel, making an incision in the abdomen.

"Pindocles, stop!"

The Greek looked up from the naked corpse. "Good evening, Centurion. To what do I owe the honor of this late visit?"

"That's the man I lost in the ambush yesterday! What in Hades are you doing to him?"

"He will be cremated in the morning. Tonight, I'm availing myself of the opportunity to learn more of human anatomy. It will make me a better doctor."

Glaxus felt his stomach turning. "You mutilate my fallen comrades to satisfy your curiosity?"

"By the time my blade enters him, he is beyond pain. You run your blade through the living, Centurion."

"I'm a soldier!"

"And I am a physician. We must both practice our craft if we wish to remain proficient, true?"

Averting his eyes from the table, Glaxus walked around it and stood before Pindocles. "The Legate knows of this?"

"I obtained his permission beforehand. His only stipulation was that the body be presentable when it is laid on the funeral pyre tomorrow. All incisions will be sewn shut when I am finished. Even the head will be stitched on. The illustrious Tridonis is most understanding when it comes to my search for knowledge."

It was well known that Tridonis held Pindocles' medical skills in high regard. This thought reminded Glaxus of why he came to the infirmary. He removed his leather money purse from his wrist and took out a silver denarius. "I know the Legate has wax-coated writing tablets made up especially for your use. I want to buy one. I have some writing to do and I don't want to use birchbark. I'd have waited until morning, but I saw the lamp through the window."

Pindocles eyed the coin closely, but didn't touch it. "My supply of tablets is not unlimited. If you will please take the letter out from under your cloak, I shall have the wax melted and reapplied, giving you a fresh surface on which to write."

Glaxus tried to control his surprise. "How did you—"

"I can see through a window as well as you, Centurion. You were in plain sight under the torch."

Glaxus reminded himself he was dealing with an intelligence superior to his own, though he considered it no embarrassment. Just as some people were physically exceptional, others were mentally so. On the other hand, he knew himself not to be an idiot. He realized the worst thing he could do when dealing with Pindocles was get flustered. "I want to save the letter for personal reasons, so melting and reapplying the wax is unacceptable. Now will you sell me a tablet?"

"No," said Pindocles, and walked away.

Glaxus took a deep breath and counted to five in his head. "Why not? I'll give you two denarii."

The Greek had padded silently to his writing table, his long, black robes making him appear to float across the floor. He came back to Glaxus and handed over a stylus and tablet. "Return the stylus when you are finished. The tablet and your coins you may keep." He picked up his scalpel and bent over the body again. "Far be it from me to block the path of true love."

"Love?" Once more Glaxus had to quell his astonishment. Was Pindocles a mind reader?

"It's a disease I have often seen before. The symptoms are less obvious in an older, steadier man such as yourself, but plain enough to a practiced eye. Now go, Centurion. Write your reply. I hope it reaches its destination and achieves the desired result."

Realizing Pindocles would sneer at any expression of thanks, Glaxus left quietly and returned directly to his quarters. Fortunately, Macro was next door, drinking and laughing loudly with Quintar's optio. Glaxus removed his cloak, then called in one of his troops from the barracks to help him off with his armor. Dismissing the soldier, he filled a lamp with olive oil and sat beneath it to write. As he did, the memories inevitably came.

He met her in Rome. He'd been transferred from Egypt to Germania and was making a stopover in the capital to see his father. It was during this visit that a long-time heart ailment finally claimed his father's life. A low-ranking assistant who'd been employed by several senators over the years, his father had died while in the service of Senator Valerius Andorus.

Unwilling to be bothered with the funeral rites of a faithful worker, the Senator sent his daughter, who graciously apologized for his absence. To Glaxus' amazement, this scion of a patrician family treated him as an equal, without a trace of condescension. Her clothing was plain and her black hair free of curls and ribbons. Unlike many upper-class women in Rome, she applied no paint around her large, dark eyes. He thought she looked the better for it.

When he asked if he might see her again, she calmly agreed. On their first outing he foolishly suggested they attend gladiator games at the Taurus Amphitheatre. Calvinia had firmly refused. "So we can watch men and animals slaughter each other? No! I don't see how Romans can enjoy such things and still call themselves civilized."

They had gone instead to the old forum to have the midday meal and to hear Athenian philosophers. She knew them all and spoke Greek fluently, joining in their arguments. "We are what we do," she told them, "and what we do is of our own free will. We are not the playthings of the gods."

She eventually revealed to Glaxus that she hadn't been married until she was twenty-three, some eight or ten years later than most Roman women. Her mother would never force her, much to her father's chagrin. After her mother's death, a union was arranged with a promising young magistrate. It lasted three years while he gambled away their savings. After he succumbed to a lung illness, she returned to her father's house, childless and destitute. That was eleven years earlier. She hadn't remarried because she felt marriage had become a farce among the patrician class.

Then Glaxus told her of how he'd been a soldier since he was twenty. Born a plebeian, he considered it a way to advance himself and see something of the world. Now, at the age of thirty-nine, he was nearing retirement. He awkwardly mentioned that he would be free to marry at that time.

She had smiled. "You are honest and good, Glaxus. I hope you find someone worthy of you."

Shortly before departing for Germania, he proposed to her, asking if she would wait till he was out of the army. She seemed distracted for a day or two before, but he hadn't thought it serious. She refused him in tears, saying she intended to marry someone else and could give no further explanation. He left Rome feeling hurt and confused, thinking that he would likely never marry. He knew her father opposed the match. The Senator had bluntly told him so in her presence. Though their fathers usually selected their first husbands, Roman women had freedom of choice in any future matches. In spite of this, Glaxus suspected the Senator's disapproval had something to do with Calvinia's refusal. Now he had been proven right.

Though it left the door open for him, her letter contained no outright declaration of love. He therefore decided that his should not. His command of written Latin was limited compared to hers, but he was confident he could make himself clear. He pressed the stylus into the wax and began.

4th of September,
762 From the City's Founding

Calvinia,

There is nothing dishonorable about owning a butcher shop. Let all the butchers and vegetable sellers of Rome close down for a day and watch how soon the patricians howl with hunger.

Thank you for telling me why you were forced to refuse me. The knowledge has been a great relief. I understand the difficulty into which your father placed you. Always remember that you bear no responsibility for the disrepute he brought upon the house of Andorus.

If I survive the campaign with Varus, I'll return to Rome at the end of my enlistment and will hope to find you pleased at my arrival. However, you are certainly under no obligation to me. Remember also that I could return with an arm or leg hacked off, which might change any feelings either of us may have. And if I am killed, I wish you a long and happy life and hope you recall me fondly.

—Glaxus

He tied the tablet shut and addressed the outside with a reed pen dipped in ink. If it reached Calvinia, it would do so around the middle of November. The campaign would be well under way by then. He slid the letter under his straw mattress an instant before Macro wobbled in and announced the obvious.

"I'm drunk, Glaxus!"

"By all the gods! Who'd have known? Does Quintar's optio share your happy condition?"

"He does!" Macro belched and sat heavily on his cot. "We put our money together and bought a jug of Setinian wine from one of the cavalrymen who rode in today. The fellow carried it here all the way from Rome!"

"So he could gouge two fools out of their hard-earned pay?"

"Of course! But it was worth it!"

"I'll need you on your toes tomorrow, no matter how much your head hurts."

Macro pulled awkwardly at his sandal straps. "A sestertius says I'm out of bed before you in the morning."

"It's a wager." Leaving on his under tunic because of the cool night, Glaxus stretched out on his cot and pulled up the woolen blanket. "And try not to snore, will you? Last time you were drunk, you sounded like the bellows of Vulcan all night."

"Another sestertius says I'm silent as the dead until sunrise."

"Agreed, but you'll have to take my word for it if you're not."

"I know how bloody truthful you are. If you tell me I snored, I'll know I did."

Macro finally managed to get his sandals off, put out the lamp, and crawl under his blanket. After a moment, he spoke to Glaxus in the dark.

"Was the letter from her? And have you written back?"

Glaxus wished he had never mentioned Calvinia to Macro. "Yes and yes," he said abruptly, expecting more intrusive questions.

But Macro only asked, "Are things hopeful?" When Glaxus said they were, he grunted his encouragement and fell asleep. He didn't snore at all and at dawn he was out of his cot first, though he had to lean against a wall for several minutes before he could get moving. Glaxus handed over the two sestertii with the advice that they not be used to buy wine. Macro nodded very slowly.

Varus arrived at the head of the column at mid-morning. Glaxus hoped to catch a glimpse of the General, but his century was put to work behind the fort. Plutarius had detailed troops all over the adjacent area to begin building an encampment for the incoming legions and civilian colonizers. In the afternoon, some of the newly arriving soldiers were sent to join the effort. They brought eagerly awaited news from Rome as well as the various provinces. For this reason, Glaxus tolerated conversation as long as it didn't impede the work. To forbid it would harm morale and create resentment. The other centurions took the same approach.

There was word of Rome's latest gladiators and charioteers, as well as the city's political developments. Glaxus was not surprised by talk of how Andorus died in disgrace after being ousted from the senate. Such a scandalous event would be a natural topic of gossip. He was relieved to hear no mention of the Senator's relatives.

There were also accounts of skirmishes in Parthia and the revolt in Pannonia, along with several unflattering reports concerning General Varus. Glaxus heard things about him that confirmed what Calvinia had written. The stories went that Varus had neither the training nor the experience to be a military commander. He was actually a converted government administrator, and a venal one at that. According to other rumors he hadn't known the proper route on the march up from Rome and needed to rely heavily on his officers. He also had the dangerous habit of letting the column stretch out too long. Glaxus didn't see how these tales could inspire confidence in the men, especially if it became necessary to fight.

In all the talking Glaxus learned that an old friend he served with in Egypt was now a senior centurion in one of Varus' legions. When they parted, Tytho was being transferred to the Judean province. It would be good to see him again after nearly five years.

As the work continued, Germanic auxiliaries were axing trees to provide lumber for a pontoon bridge across the Rhine. Nearby, Glaxus and his century were digging defensive trenches and building earthen ramparts. He grimaced at how much effort it took to force the shovel into the hard, cold ground. Plutarius once disapproved of his going beyond supervision to work with the troops. "You did enough of that before becoming a senior centurion. You've now earned the right to lead by word instead of deed." Glaxus had replied there was still no better way to lead than by example. He pointed out that Alexander the Great always did so.

Plutarius had snorted in disgust. "When that Macedonian bandit died 332 years ago, his empire promptly fell. A good thing, because if it hadn't, Rome's couldn't have risen. But his had to collapse after his death because it was founded only on the power of his personality. Our empire is founded on obedience, patriotism, and discipline, on the willingness of each of us to subordinate our uniqueness for the sake of the whole. Doing manual labor with your men is more ostentation than example. You should chasten yourself and refrain from it. Consider my advice carefully."

Glaxus considered it and decided to continue as he had. He was aware his fellow centurions and their optios didn't like seeing him do it any more than Plutarius did. Until he was ordered not to, however, he would work with the men. Macro was not enthusiastic about joining him in this, but always did so.

Near day's end, a soldier came to Glaxus with a written message from the Legate. It was an order to have Arminius report to headquarters.

"What does this concern?"

"I haven't been told, Centurion. I know only that he is to come immediately."

There was obviously nothing to do but obey. "Arminius, this soldier has brought an order summoning you to headquarters. Go."

"Yes sir." Arminius climbed out of the trench and went into the fort.

Was Arminius to be given his auxiliary command now? It seemed very early, but perhaps Varus had brought new orders from the Emperor. Glaxus hoped such was the case. Arminius was a superior soldier, but his singular status was a burden no centurion needed. Let him go on to his special destiny, whatever it might be.

Shortly before sunset, enough entrenchments had been prepared to allow the first leather tents to be pitched. This process continued by torchlight until the end of the night's second watch. Glaxus and his century assisted up to then. He'd told his men it was vital to have temporary quarters ready for the arriving legions. They responded well, and by order of the Chief Centurion were given the first half of the following day to rest.

"Your soldiers deserve it." Plutarius observed Glaxus' mud-spattered armor. "By following your . . . your example, they outworked most of the other centuries."

Glaxus knew better than to laugh or even smile. "They work for the spirit of the legion, sir. I merely guide them in doing so. As you said, there's no room for individual personality in the Roman army."

"So I did, though General Varus wouldn't seem to agree." Plutarius frowned and shook his head. "May the gods protect us."

Glaxus didn't like the sound of this. The night's third watch had begun and he and the Chief Centurion were walking to their quarters. The torch lit assembly ground was deserted but for the two of them.

"Is there something about the General you find disquieting, sir?"

"Yes. Varus is arrogant and eager for personal glory. He has nothing but contempt for the Gauls and their ways. He displayed that in war council today with the Legate and the tribunes."

"War council already? His entire force won't arrive and be encamped for another day."

"He's in a hurry. Segestes and Arminius were also there."

"Yes, I received the order to send Arminius. Has he been made a commander in the auxiliaries?"

"He has. An infantry commander. Varus brought the final order giving him that rank and granting him Roman citizenship. The original plan was to wait for successful colonization, but Augustus changed his mind. I'm sure the Emperor is impatient to see the colony established and the Germanic tribes completely Romanized. Since Varus wants to impress the Emperor, he's eager to get it done, no matter who he angers along the way. Today he told the two Gauls their people were inferior savages. When war council was over and the General had left, the Legate and I tried to apologize for him. Only Segestes seemed willing to let it pass easily. Arminius needed some coaxing from his father-in-law before agreeing to forget it."

Glaxus recalled Quintar's remarks about Rome assuming too much.

"I'm sure you're relieved to be rid of Arminius," the Chief Centurion continued, "but you should know that he mentioned you by name at the council today. He told us you taught him much during his short time in your century. Such praise will make the Legate want to commend you face-to-face."

Glaxus knew that Tridonis occasionally talked directly to individual soldiers, sometimes even the lowliest legionary. This was unusual for a legate, but having risen from their ranks, he displayed an affinity for his troops that the tribunes no doubt considered disgusting.

"I'd be honored to speak with the Legate," replied Glaxus.

Plutarius fixed a steady gaze on him. "Are you sure you want to retire after this campaign? I plan to, but I'm fifteen years older than you."

Glaxus hadn't heard about this. "I wasn't aware you were retiring, sir."

"Yes, thirty-six years of army life is enough. But of course a new chief centurion for the legion will have to be named before I leave."

Glaxus wasn't sure how to respond to this. "Yes sir. Of course."

Plutarius laughed. "Come now, Glaxus! You know damn well you'd be up for consideration if you don't retire. You're only nearing forty. What would you do outside the army at that age? Be a farmer? Or a civil servant, taking pay for doing nothing? Or perhaps run a shop of some kind with a wife by your side, the two of you getting old and fat together. None of that is fit for a soldier!"

Glaxus flinched at these words, but kept silent.

"The army needs your experience and could reward you for it handsomely." Plutarius stopped walking and turned Glaxus toward the headquarters building. "That's your next step up. Do well in there and you may even follow the same route as Tridonis. The odds are against it, but it's possible."

"There are others as well qualified, sir."

"Some come close, such as Quintar, but you'd be at the top of the list."

Glaxus looked at headquarters for a moment, then closed his eyes and saw Calvinia.

But he quickly opened them again. This was a chance that had to be considered. One soldier in a hundred became a centurion, one in twelve hundred a senior centurion, but barely one in six thousand became chief centurion of a legion. And he hadn't yet sent the letter. He could easily write another, telling her of the opportunity he'd been given. Wouldn't she want him to reach the pinnacle of his profession?

"What do you say, Glaxus? Do I tell the Legate you want to be considered?"

"Sir, please tell the Legate that I am retiring after this campaign and returning to Rome. I have personal business there."

Plutarius was visibly disappointed. "You're the one I'd have recommended. You're the best."

"Thank you, Chief Centurion, but that's my final decision."

"Would you like to give me a better idea as to why?"

"You've reached your limit at thirty-six years, sir. I've reached mine at twenty. There are things I wish to know in life besides the army, and a man has only so much time."

"That's a fact, and with Varus in charge of our lives, time may . . ." Plutarius shook his head. "Good night, my friend."

"Good night, sir."

Glaxus watched the Chief Centurion cross the assembly ground to his private room in the headquarters building. He was one of the truly revered soldiers in the legions, his advice highly prized by Tridonis. A recommendation from him would doubtlessly make Glaxus his successor.

But Glaxus had resolved to retire even before receiving Calvinia's letter. Two decades of fighting, wounds, and narrow escapes from death were enough. If he accepted the promotion, he'd be committing himself to several more years. And now, he'd possibly be turning his back on Calvinia. He wouldn't do that.

He began thinking about tomorrow's duties. After their morning off, his century was scheduled to spend the afternoon digging sanitation holes for the incoming legions and settlers. He chuckled aloud as he approached the barracks. This was one of those times he'd get bantered by the other centurions for wanting to work with his men.

"Laughing to yourself, Glaxus? That's a bad sign."

He looked up to see a short, stocky centurion standing in the barracks door. "Tytho! You old war-horse! I heard you were coming!"

"And I heard you were here!" Tytho exchanged a right forearm clasp with Glaxus. "I asked around and found your barracks."

"What legion are you with? The 17th?"

"The 18th. I command the third century in the fifth cohort."

"Come inside," said Glaxus. "We'll talk awhile."

The barracks was nearly empty. Having the next morning off, most of the century quickly got cleaned up and left with Macro. There had been word that traveling brothels arrived with the new legions. Glaxus suspected that was where they'd gone.

He sat on his cot while Tytho sat on Macro's. They took their helmets off and in the lamplight Glaxus saw that his friend's face had been burned dark brown.

"The Judean sun certainly left its mark on you. Did your service there go well?"

"Well enough, though the people grumble against Rome constantly. They call us gentile dogs and say we worship false gods."

Glaxus shrugged. "Is there anyone who believes in all the gods all the time?"

"I did before I went to Judea. You know, the Jews think there's only one god. After being exposed to it for awhile, it makes you wonder."

"When I was last in Rome, I met Athenian philosophers who say there may be no gods at all."

"Philosophers!" Tytho didn't disguise his contempt. "They're all charlatans and liars! I saw a Judean boy about twelve years old that would put them all to shame. His articulation and depth of thought would have astounded old Plato himself."

"When was this?"

"Four years ago. I was leading a patrol past the Jews' temple when I saw him talking with some of their sages. He was surprising all who heard him. I had learned quite a bit of Aramaic by then and wanted to ask his name, but Jews won't speak to Romans if they can help it. When his parents came to get him, they were upset because he had wandered away from them. His answer was something about needing to do his father's business. It was an odd thing to say, since his father was right there and not very pleased with him."

"You never heard of him again?" asked Glaxus.

"No. Wherever he is, he'd be about sixteen by now."

It was another hour before they stopped talking. Tytho wanted to hear what soldiering was like in Germany and how tough the Gauls were to fight. He finally went to his tent, leaving Glaxus to think that with the morning off, it was a chance to sleep past dawn for once.

But first, he reached under his mattress and pulled out the letter to Calvinia. Stepping into the barracks hall, he put it with the birchbark letters written by his men. The mail would be bagged and dispatched to Rome in the next day or two. He stood silently for a moment, hoping that whatever gods there might be, they would guide his words into her hands. He then returned to his quarters and went to bed.

"Centurion! Wake up!"

Glaxus heaved out of sleep to find one of the arrogant young tribunes standing over him. He believed this one was called Fabius. Macro and Quintar were in the doorway, appearing strangely eager.

Something was astir. Why would an officer of such rank come into a barracks to speak with a centurion? Why not use a messenger? This was also Glaxus' first direct contact with any of the six tribunes attached to the 19th Legion. He immediately threw off his blanket and got to his feet.

"Sir?"

"The Chief Centurion tells me you've led many patrols in the surrounding area and are very familiar with the forests. Is that true?"

Glaxus wondered if the Gauls had broken the alliance.

"Answer me!"

"Yes sir, that's true."

Fabius pulled Glaxus' ring mail shirt off its hook and threw it upon the cot. "Then get into your armor and report to headquarters at once! You will accompany us on the bear hunt!"

III

In his impatience, Fabius was virtually shouting. "I must find three of the largest bears in Germania! General Varus has promised to send them to Rome for gladiator games the Emperor is presenting in November. The General has honored me with the task of capturing them and you will lend your assistance. Senior Centurion Quintar has volunteered his century to provide the manpower. Your optio also asked to join us."

Ambition, realized Glaxus. Fabius was young and plainly anxious for advancement. In fact, he probably had to compete with the other tribunes for this chance to ingratiate himself with Varus and the Emperor. But such behavior was certainly not confined to tribunes. Macro wanted to join the Praetorian Guard and Quintar had probably learned he was being considered for Chief Centurion. Volunteering for this assignment could help them toward those goals. Such was the way of the world and always would be. A few years ago, Glaxus might have had the same idea. Now, he thought of how Calvinia would react if she knew he was helping to satisfy the bloodlust of Rome.

"Sir, Centurion Quintar and Optio Macro know the countryside as well as I. They would be more than sufficient to—"

"You're coming! Plutarius says you know the territory better than anyone. He also claims you can throw a javelin through a marble slab. I need the bears alive, but if we absolutely have to kill one to protect somebody's life, we'll . . . we'll do so."

Glaxus wasn't sure he believed that.

"Now arm yourself and report posthaste!" Fabius brushed between Macro and Quintar on his way out.

Glaxus sighed and began to put on his ring mail. Macro stepped over to help him.

Quintar smiled broadly. "You should be flattered, Glaxus. Plutarius told the Tribune there could be no better guide for such an expedition than you. Besides, this will be quite an adventure, don't you think?"

"Only a couple of days ago you said Rome was overreaching and asked me what the world might be like without the empire. You seem to have regained your enthusiasm about being part of it."

"Yes, and I have you to thank. Now that you've refused the position of Chief Centurion, they're thinking of me. If I can be of assistance on this hunt, that may secure things for me. But why decline a promotion that was yours for the taking?"

"He has his reasons." Macro was behind Glaxus, pulling down the ring mail. "Besides, he has nothing to prove. There isn't anything he hasn't done in the army."

"I've never hunted bears. How did this come about?"

Quintar explained. "Fabius says that at last evening's meal, Varus mentioned his promise to the Emperor and asked for a volunteer to fulfill it on his behalf. Tridonis thought it a waste of time, but could do nothing about it. The tribunes soon got into an argument about who would have the glory of the hunt, and the General finally chose Fabius. Late last night, Plutarius summoned me and told me of your decision, Glaxus. He asked me if I wanted to be considered and I said yes. He and I then learned of the hunt and I quickly requested to go along. Preparations for it have been underway all night. Just this morning Plutarius suggested to the Tribune that you accompany us as well. On the way over here, Fabius and I met Macro returning from the brothels."

"And when Quintar said I was the Optio of the Centurion they were looking for, I naturally asked the Tribune how I might be of assistance. Fabius was a Praetorian Guardsman for a year and has many friends among them."

Glaxus couldn't resist a slight smile. "I see."

"Yes, so when I found out what was happening, I also asked to go. While we were walking over, Quintar and I fell behind the Tribune a little to talk. He told me you turned down the job of Chief Centurion and that he had good hopes of getting it after the colonization campaign."

"But you haven't told me why you refused it, and if Macro knows, he won't say."

As Macro finished pulling on the ring mail, Glaxus put a hand on his shoulder. "My optio is loyal. Would you want yours to be otherwise?"

Quintar laughed. "No, I wouldn't."

Before they started for headquarters, Glaxus selected from the armory two javelins with non-bending shafts. Outside, the sun was just rising. He thought again of Calvinia and hoped she would understand that he had no choice. The only thing to do was get it over with while making sure, if he could, that no one was hurt. But then he wasn't in command of this escapade. Fabius was.

Glaxus turned his mind now to bears. He'd seen them only in amphitheatres, but of their presence in the Germanic forests there was no question. He had come across their spoor more than once while on patrol. The Gauls in the auxiliary units occasionally spoke of them as being large, brown, and fierce.

"How exactly are we supposed to do this?" he asked. "I hope the Tribune has a plan."

"He does," said Quintar. "Hounds will chase down the bears and corner them, then we'll get them under control with ropes and nets and put them in crates."

"So they can go to Rome to be butchered?"

Quintar stared at Glaxus. "It's what the Emperor wants. Besides, they're only stupid animals. What else are they good for?"

"Right," agreed Macro. "And there's always more of them anyway."

Glaxus wondered how long that would be so.

They reached headquarters only to learn that Fabius was supervising the loading of the crates onto wagons. This process could be heard going on just outside the fort's walls, the baying of hounds mixing with the Tribune's shouted orders. Glaxus glanced around. He wanted to ask Plutarius why he had been needlessly recommended for the hunt, but the Chief Centurion was nowhere in sight.

Peering down the dim central hallway, Glaxus noticed Arminius standing close to the wall. He was wearing the insignia of his new rank, an auxiliary infantry commander. Clinging to his arm was a young woman wearing a full-length leather dress. She was probably his wife, the daughter of Segestes. Pointing to Glaxus and the others, she whispered in Arminius' ear and he led her toward them.

Glaxus could see that she was certainly a Germanic Gaul. She had long blonde hair worn in two braids, a fair complexion, and blue eyes. But as she was only about sixteen, there was no character in her face. It was just a pretty little mask. He wouldn't have taken it in trade for the maturity and experience of Calvinia's face.

As Arminius approached, he met Glaxus' eyes. "Greetings, Centurion."

"Greetings, Commander Arminius."

"Actually, I prefer Herman now, my Germanic name."

This was followed by an awkward pause during which Macro and Quintar gaped at the new commander.

"Germanic name? But wasn't he one of yours, Glaxus?"

Macro answered Quintar's question. "Yes, he was. What's going on?"

Glaxus knew trouble was coming, but wasn't sure how to avoid it. "Commander Herman was discreetly put under my charge to get some experience in Roman military techniques before being promoted."

"Is she your wife?" demanded Quintar.

Herman pulled her a little closer. "She is."

"A Germanic Gaul allowed to enlist in a regular legion, and married as well? Then promoted to an auxiliary command after only a few months' service?" Quintar scowled. "Something stinks about this."

"There's been some deal making!" snapped Macro. "What's the story, you Gaulish—"

"Silence!" ordered Glaxus. "The Optio will show the Commander the respect due his rank!"

"Yes sir." But Macro's glare was locked on Herman.

In the tense moment that followed, Glaxus waited for Herman's explanation, but apparently the Gaul felt none was owed. After all, hadn't he risked his life on patrol only a few days ago and nearly been killed? Still, his smug silence wasn't helping. He seemed different from the young legionary he had been. Was this his new personality? Or the original one?

"Is it for us to oppose the Emperor's arrangements? He commands, we obey." Glaxus hoped saying this would tell Quintar and Macro all they needed to know, at least until he could talk to them privately. He realized he should have mentioned it on the walk over from the barracks, but had forgotten it in his surprise about the bear hunt.

Quintar clearly understood. "We'll speak later," he told Glaxus evenly. "Your optio and I will go assist Tribune Fabius."

Macro also appeared to comprehend, but made no apology to Herman, speaking instead to Glaxus. "Forgive my outburst, Centurion." He then followed Quintar.

After Macro stepped out the door, Herman addressed Glaxus. "You hunt the Brown Ones today?"

"Yes."

"The forest was their home before it was ours. Now you take them away from it so they can die in Rome for the amusement of the Emperor?"

"I would gladly leave them be, but as the Commander knows, the will of Augustus is what matters. I was ordered to participate and must do so to the best of my ability."

"If no one obeyed Augustus, his will would be meaningless."

"People must live in some kind of society, which requires an authority to maintain it. The Roman Emperor is that authority."

"My ancestors lived here in societies of their own making long before there was a Rome."

To Glaxus, this prompted an obvious question. "If you disapprove of Roman authority and society, why do you serve in the Roman army and accept Roman citizenship?"

"Who said I disapproved? Good luck catching the Emperor's bears. I hope they give him a fine show and take some gladiators with them when they die." Herman then spoke to his wife in Germanic. She answered softly, untying from around her neck a strip of leather she'd been wearing under her dress. On it hung a small wooden figure of a bear. She shyly handed it to Glaxus.

"My wife's name is Thusnelda. She wishes you to have that. It will keep you safe on the hunt. She says you're not as arrogant as Varus and Fabius, nor as hostile as Macro and Quintar. I've also told her how you unselfishly gave up the gold armbands. She wonders why someone like you would consort with such as those."

"They have their faults, but Macro and Quintar are still my friends. If this is not meant for them as well, I cannot accept it. But, I thank you."

Herman grinned wryly and spoke to Thusnelda in their native tongue. She frowned as Glaxus returned the amulet to her.

"I knew you'd refuse it," said her husband. "You're too Roman to be believed, Centurion."

"So are you, Commander." As Glaxus left, he noted how startled Herman was by this reply.

Outside the fort all appeared to be ready. The crates and rolled-up nets had been tied onto ox-drawn wagons. Most of Quintar's men were assuming marching formation while others gripped rope leashes, restraining the large pack of hounds. Fabius sat on his horse at the head of the century, talking with the group of cavalry officers that attended him. He soon noticed Glaxus.

"Centurion! Come here!"

"Sir?"

"We've been discussing the best area in which to stage the hunt. Where do you suggest?"

"I've seen bear tracks many times while patrolling in the forest a few miles west of the fort. A well-worn marching trail leads directly there."

"Good. Let's proceed."

"But I cannot guarantee that bears will be in the vicinity, Tribune. We may have to try two or three areas before we find any."

"We'll find some if I have to burn down the forest to do it. I'm not returning empty-handed!"

Concerned by the increasing intensity in Fabius' manner, Glaxus tried to reply in a calming voice. "If we fail today, sir, we may have better fortune later. Surely the General and the Emperor know how difficult this—"

"If I fail today, another Tribune will be given the chance in my place. I'll not let this opportunity slip away. We're returning with bears, Centurion. Is that clear?"

"Extremely clear, sir."

"It had better be. Now, walk beside my horse to guide us."

A few minutes later they were on the right trail. Glaxus then began marching on the century's left while Quintar took the right. Macro and Quintar's optio marched at the rear. No one spoke, by order of Fabius. Glaxus thought this ridiculous, considering the hounds never ceased barking and baying. Any bears out there would be warned well in advance.

As they marched, a thick fog descended to the treetops. Glaxus hoped it wouldn't drop to ground level. Chasing through the woods after bears was dangerous enough. Having to do so while unable to see your next step would be madness. And of course, there were the Gauls. What if a tribe that rejected the alliance was out hunting today in the same territory? He pulled his cloak over his shoulders and shook his head in dismay. This expedition was poorly planned and in too much of a hurry.

But duty was duty. Glaxus therefore watched carefully for a certain bend in the trail. When he saw it, he immediately went to Fabius and pointed to the left.

The Tribune halted the formation and peered into the dim forest. "Here?"

"Yes sir. I've seen tracks on this trail and in that section of the woods. Berry bushes grow in there. From what the Gauls say, that's one of the things bears like to eat."

A cavalry officer who had ridden several yards ahead called out that he'd found paw prints. Fabius rode to the spot with Glaxus loping alongside. The hounds were howling madly and straining at their leashes.

Displaying long claw marks, the prints were large and fresh. They were also very deep. That led Glaxus to believe the bear had been running when it crossed the trail, probably because it heard the hounds. He mentioned this to Fabius.

"If it's running from me, Centurion, then I've got to be after it! Unleash the pack! We on horses will ride behind them! When we have it cornered, we'll send someone back for the nets and ropes!"

With the hounds charging into the brush, Fabius whirled his stallion around to follow them. Glaxus wanted to tell him that plowing through the forest's undergrowth on horseback would be impossible, but there was only time to let him find out for himself. He was just three yards off the trail before he quickly retreated, swearing viciously at the briar that cut into his legs.

The Tribune leaped to the ground, obviously trying to hide his chagrin. "New plan! The dogs alone can run the bear down and keep it trapped while we follow on foot with the equipment. I want Senior Centurions Glaxus and Quintar along with Optio Macro and half the century. The other half will wait here. They'll get their turn on the next bear. We'll also see what the horse soldiers can do when they're on two feet instead of four. Now make ready!"

The cavalry officers reluctantly dismounted and gathered around Fabius. Quintar quickly chose half his century, then ordered them to pull the nets and ropes off the wagons. Glaxus removed his cloak, explaining that it would only get in the way. Fabius agreed and ordered everyone to do the same.

"We'll freeze!" muttered Macro.

"Don't you want to be a Praetorian?" whispered Quintar.

"Yes sir. As much as you want to be a chief centurion."

"Then take it off and freeze."

Such talk from his comrades bothered Glaxus. "For now we must forget future prospects and think only of the task before us. Remain alert, stay with the group, and no individual heroics to impress Fabius. Understood?"

Macro and Quintar glanced at each other, then nodded to Glaxus.

As he had in the past, Glaxus found his shield useful in pushing through the briar and other undergrowth in the forest. There were also areas where the ground between the trees was clear, allowing them to run at half-speed. However, much of the clear terrain was hilly, making Fabius angry because it slowed them down. The baying of the pack floated clearly on the damp air, leading them in a direction Glaxus determined was roughly northwest. The territory was familiar. He figured they'd come about a mile from their starting point on the trail.

Moments later, the fog began to drop. Unable to see the men at the back, he asked Fabius' permission to check on them.

"Permission granted, but don't tarry. The dogs sound close."

Glaxus trotted around the formation. There were no stragglers, but at the rear the men burdened with nets and ropes were starting to tire. He was about to have them switch their loads to other soldiers when he heard by the barking that the dogs had stopped. This was followed by the shouting of Fabius.

"Everyone forward! Don't let it escape!"

The formation surged ahead, pulling away from Glaxus and the equipment-laden men. "Do your best!" he told them, and they staggered after him as he began running. Only yards away, Fabius' commands could barely be heard above the frenzied barking.

"Keep your javelins leveled at it! Surround it!"

Despite the fog, Glaxus could make out a small clearing ahead. The shadowy figures of men and hounds were visible, darting about in furious activity. Squinting through the gloom, he saw another shadow, huge and unmistakable. It made a quick swiping motion and a dog was raked off the ground, whining in agony before dropping limply in Glaxus' path. He hopped over the body and reached Fabius' side at the clearing.

Towering above the dogs on its hind legs, the bear stood with its back against a large pine. Glaxus estimated its size at two and half yards tall and a thousand pounds. Bawling at the hounds, it held its front paws ready to punish any more that got too close. Glaxus knew time was short. Either the pack would rush it all at once and kill it, or it would break into the woods and the chase would start over.

The troops bearing the equipment were just now reaching the clearing. "Tribune!" Glaxus shouted. "We must get the nets on it at once!"

"No! The ropes first in case the nets don't hold it!"

"But, sir—"

"You heard me!"

Dropping their shields and javelins, Glaxus and Quintar grabbed ropes with looped ends. On the clearing's opposite side Macro stood several yards to the bear's right. His spear tip was one of many aimed at it, everyone being around the clearing by now. But would Fabius really order the men to throw if necessary? Forcing this thought away, Glaxus drew a deep breath and stepped forward with Quintar.

"Closer! You mustn't miss!"

Wishing the Tribune would either cast a rope or shut up, Glaxus shifted the loop to his right hand and took another step.

The noise from the hounds was deafening. When one brushed against his leg, he nearly lost his footing.

They had come within five paces of the bear. Just as it fixed its eyes on him, Glaxus tossed his loop. Quintar tossed his at the same time, but both passed over its head as it dropped onto four paws. Spinning to the left, it slipped under the javelins of the cavalry officers on that side. Several were knocked down, one wailing horribly as the fleeing animal stepped squarely in his crotch.

Hounds and troops were instantly in pursuit. Glaxus seized one of his javelins and started running. Quintar was beside him, still carrying a rope. Fabius lagged a few steps behind, shouting orders no one seemed to hear in the mad dash through the forest.

"There's a river ahead!" yelled Glaxus. "If it reaches deep water, we've lost it!"

He and Quintar broke clear of the trees in time to see the bear reach the water's edge and charge into the shallows. The dogs went in after it. One bit into its shoulder and was gutted by a single blow. Another was sent flying with a broken spine.

Glaxus looked around for the nets, but the men carrying them had fallen behind again. "Quintar!" he called. "The rope!" Though Quintar's toss fell cleanly over the bear's head, the creature's huge jaws sheared through the loop like a thread.

Fabius shoved his way around Glaxus and ran into the river. Passing the bear by less than two yards, the Tribune attempted to cut off its escape into deeper water. When he shouted for assistance, the men closest to him hesitated. Only Macro rushed to his side. They lowered their javelins at the bear and managed to bluff it into stopping. Fabius shouted for the nets, which were only now arriving.

Gripping his javelin with one hand, Glaxus helped Quintar and several others carry a net into the frigid river. Glaxus was appalled at how close Macro and Fabius were to the bear. Two ambitious fools whose desire for advancement could get them both killed! Was the Emperor's pleasure worth that?

Spinning in circles, the bear appeared stymied and indecisive. The hounds were staying just out of its reach while three men had joined Fabius and Macro. Glaxus knew there wouldn't be a better chance to use a net, but when Fabius saw them bringing one over, he tried to drive the bear that way. "Go!" he yelled at it. "Go on!"

"No, Tribune! Keep your distance! Let us come to the bear to make our throw!" When they'd taken two more paces, Glaxus decided they were within range. "Now!"

But Fabius suddenly advanced and prodded the animal's rump. Whirling about, it ran from under the falling net and bit his javelin in two. In one lunge it was on him, its front paws pressing him underwater and face first into the gravel below.

Coming to the Tribune's aid, Macro thrust his javelin into the bear's shoulder and was hurled aside by a stroke of its left paw. Quintar drew his sword and plunged the blade into its flank. Roaring with fury and pain, it reared on its hind legs and turned, jerking the weapon from his grasp. Attempting to run, he tripped over a hound and became entangled in the floating net.

"Glaxus! I'm caught!"

Glaxus gritted his teeth and placed himself between Quintar and the enraged bear. He sought to ram his javelin through its stomach, but couldn't avoid its right paw. Caught squarely in the chest by the blow, he was knocked backwards in a tumble. Below the surface for an instant, he broke into the air with a gasp and found himself unhurt.

The bear had snatched up Quintar. He was screaming as it crushed him against its chest, a score of javelins bouncing off its muscled body. Glaxus fumbled frantically in the murky shallows for his own javelin. He felt his fingers close around it and leaped to his feet, judging his distance from the bear at ten paces.

Cursing Fabius, he brought his arm back and locked his eyes on a spot in the center of the bear's throat. As the javelin left his hand, he knew he'd never thrown one harder. The iron tipped shaft sped over the water and struck the bear on target, impaling it through the neck. Without making a sound, the great beast went limp and collapsed onto Quintar.

Glaxus splashed his way forward. "Get it off him!" As a dozen soldiers rolled back the carcass, he pulled his friend clear, but saw there was no hope. Quintar was dead.

Glaxus looked angrily toward the spot where Fabius had gone under. Two cavalry officers were helping him up. He was spitting water and bleeding from deep scratches on his face, but he was alive. He groaned when lifted and complained tearfully of cracked ribs.

Macro stumbled over to the bear with a bloody hand on his left eye. "My collarbone is broken, Glaxus, and I gouged my eye on a submerged stump when the bear knocked me back." He leaned across the carcass and saw Quintar. "Oh no! By Jupiter's throne, we made a mess of things!"

"That we did." Glaxus had to keep himself from glaring at Fabius. He gently lifted Quintar and turned to some soldiers who had brought a net stretched between two javelins. He eased the body onto it and folded the arms over the chest. "Macro, you and the Tribune will be carried to the wagons on nets also." There was a shriek from the forest and Glaxus remembered the officer whose groin had been crushed. "And him. We must return to—"

"You killed my bear!" sobbed Fabius.

His resentment mingling with disgust, Glaxus felt his hand sliding up to his sword as he faced the Tribune.

"No, Glaxus!" hissed Macro. "Think!"

Stopped by these words, he managed to regain his self-control. Nodding at Macro, he then spoke calmly to Fabius. "We were all casting javelins, Tribune. I was lucky enough to hit a vulnerable spot. After the bear pushed you under, Quintar and Macro forced it away from you. The Senior Centurion was killed and my optio badly injured. You're hurt, as well. We must return to the fort immediately. Further hunting is impossible."

Fabius stared vacantly at Glaxus, then at the bear. After a moment, he began muttering in a low voice to the pair of officers holding him. They regarded him gravely as he spoke.

"But sir," said one, "it's not as though you lost a battle."

"Isn't it? I'll seem like a fool to the General. Especially if another tribune succeeds where I couldn't. Now do as I say!"

There was absolute quiet as the officers carried Fabius to the riverbank. The young soldiers all stood by numbly, their gazes fixed on the Tribune. Glaxus realized this was something they never expected to witness. He'd been in the army nearly twenty years and hadn't seen it before.

And couldn't believe there was any reason to see it now. "You must not do this, Tribune."

Fabius winced as the officers removed his battered ring mail. "Silence!"

"Excuse me, sir, but I will speak." The hypocrisy of objecting didn't escape Glaxus. His feelings of a moment ago were not forgotten. Yet Quintar had been as ambitious as Fabius and had eagerly volunteered for the hunt. "I ask you to reconsider. There may be other opportunities to earn advancement in the coming campaign."

"Other opportunities! Who would willingly follow me into combat knowing the future Chief Centurion died under my command, his life snuffed out just as he was reaching the pinnacle of his career?"

Glaxus tried to think of what Calvinia would say to Fabius. "You're not even twenty-five. You could return to Rome and study law, rhetoric, or politics. Doing this helps no one."

"You suddenly show different feathers. A moment ago you wanted to cut out my liver yourself. It was in your face for all to see." Fabius wobbled on his feet as he tossed his helmet aside and drew his sword. "You'll get your chance anyway. Come hold this for me."

Glaxus was sickened. "Sir, perhaps one of the cavalry officers would—"

"You! Now!"

Knowing there was nothing to do but get it over with, Glaxus waded to the riverbank and stepped out of the water in front of

Fabius. Taking the sword's hilt tightly in both hands, he got down on his right knee while bracing the pommel on his left. He drew in a deep breath.

"Ready, Tribune."

Fabius stared at the blade while Glaxus suddenly became aware of their surroundings. The river flowed loudly, birds sang, and shafts of sunlight reached through the trees as the fog lifted. This was a beautiful place, or had been until the Roman army came to do the Emperor's bidding.

"Uff!" Fabius emitted a loud groan as he sagged across Glaxus' knee, the reddened sword blade sprouting from his back.

Glaxus lowered the body to the ground and stood up. "The Tribune has done what he felt he had to. His corpse and that of Quintar will be returned to the fort for burning. Let us make ready and go."

As Glaxus helped Macro to a net, he felt his optio grab his arm. "With only one eye I'll have to be discharged. My career has ended, but yours has not. Quintar is gone, so there's no one at hand besides you who's qualified to be the new Chief Centurion. You may be asked again."

"The answer would be the same."

"Should it be? Perhaps this happened for a reason, Glaxus. It may be that your future isn't marriage and retirement in Rome. Perhaps the gods whisper in your ear of a grander destiny."

"They can shout if they like. I've made up my mind."

But when the return march was nearly over and the fort in sight, Glaxus caught himself wondering if the mail had been dispatched.

IV

It was mid-morning when Glaxus walked wearily into his barracks to find it mostly quiet. Several of his men were asleep on their cots. The only activity was a soldier from another century placing the mail into woolen bags. Glaxus saw that the tablet bearing his letter to Calvinia had yet to be touched.

The soldier noticed him and froze.

"At ease. You're part of the mail detachment?"

"Yes sir. We start for Rome this afternoon."

"Very well. Continue."

"Yes sir."

But as the soldier reached for the tablet, Glaxus suddenly picked it up and turned away. Why was he wavering again? Were Macro and Plutarius right? Did the gods intend him for grander things? And if he left the army, would he only grow old and soft in a childless marriage begun too late? Could he leave now, when real power was his for the taking? Perhaps he was meant to be a chief centurion, or even a legate. And why had he returned just in time to see the mail being collected? He thought little of omens, but could this truly be one?

Or was it a test?

The soldier was slipping the birchbark letters into the bags and had nearly finished. Glaxus reached out to drop the tablet into the last bag. "And that."

"Yes sir. Anything more, Centurion?"

"That's all. Good journey to Rome."

"Thank you, sir."

The young man tied the bags shut and slung them over his shoulder. Glaxus watched as they were carried across the assembly ground to headquarters. "I'm committed to her now," he said aloud, and the realization brought him an intense feeling of relief. Even if he didn't survive the upcoming campaign, he would die knowing he hadn't abandoned her.

He took off his helmet and went into his quarters. He was unbuckling his sword when his eye fell on the stylus Pindocles loaned him to write the letter.

"Damn that Greek bastard! He'd better not!"

Snatching up the stylus, Glaxus strode out of the barracks. He berated himself for not thinking of this when they got back. The cavalry officers had volunteered to take the injured to the infirmary. Macro then urged him to get some rest and they would talk later. Only now had it occurred to him that the dead would likely be taken to the infirmary also.

Drinian's body had been taken there after the ambush.

Upon entering the infirmary, Glaxus quickly glanced around. Macro was lying on a table, surrounded by Pindocles and two assistants. The bodies of Fabius and Quintar were on tables at the back of the room, covered by blankets. The moans of the man with the crushed groin were coming from somewhere out of sight.

Two of the cavalry officers were standing near the wall and Glaxus joined them in silently watching. When Pindocles went to his desk to consult one of his scrolls, Glaxus followed him.

"A word with you, physician."

"What is it now, Centurion? Your optio requires my skills."

"I won't detain you." Glaxus set the stylus on the desk. "I want only to return this, and also to ask that you not use Quintar's body to . . . further your knowledge of human anatomy."

"He was a friend of yours?"

"He was."

As Pindocles raised his angular face, Glaxus thought he saw a hint of compassion in it. "They are to be cremated an hour before sundown today. I promise you Quintar will not be touched until that time, and then only to prepare him for burning. Sufficient?"

Pindocles was cold-blooded and arrogant, but Glaxus didn't judge him to be a liar. "Sufficient. Now tell me about Macro. Can you save his eye?"

"There is nothing to save. However, his collarbone can be reassembled and will heal with time."

"The other man had his crotch stepped on by the bear. What of him?"

"He's in the rear room awaiting surgery. His genitals have been ruined and must be removed. I've given him a nostrum in unmixed wine to deaden his senses, but there will still be some pain when I begin to cut." Pindocles set the scroll down and picked up another. "Two men dead, two others permanently crippled, and the expedition returns bearless. A bad day, Centurion."

Glaxus had to agree. "Bad enough."

"A day of poor choices from what your optio tells me, though he says you accomplished your usual valiant deeds."

"I accomplished nothing. Now put my friend back together as best you can and tell him I'll see him later."

"As you wish. But one question, if I may." Pindocles pointed a bony finger at the covered bodies. "Would you also like me to refrain from anatomical explorations on Tribune Fabius?"

Glaxus swallowed his answer and walked out.

The stone platform used for funeral pyres had cooled off since Drinian's cremation. Fresh wood was stacked on it by Quintar's century under the supervision of his former optio, now promoted to Junior Centurion. Glaxus attended with Plutarius as the body was carried out and set in place. The century stood at attention while the wood was torched. Because the air was damp with fog, the fire had to be restarted twice before it fully took hold.

"Quintar doesn't want to go," remarked Plutarius.

After the body was consumed, the ashes were placed in a marble urn. "He was from Sicilia," Glaxus told the new centurion. "He once said he had a brother in Syracuse. Send the urn there."

The cremation of Fabius was to be more elaborate. While they waited for the platform to be cleared and stacked with more wood, Glaxus spoke to Plutarius.

"This is the first chance I've had to ask you why you recommended me for the bear hunt, sir."

"Haven't you guessed? In the hope that you would distinguish yourself in the eyes of Varus, and that he might then ask you to be Chief Centurion. How could you say no to the General? It would be like saying no to the Emperor himself."

"Sir, being promoted to Chief Centurion is not possible no matter who asks me. As I've explained to you, I have other plans, and I've mailed a letter committing myself to those plans."

Plutarius pulled a writing tablet from beneath his cloak. "This letter?"

Glaxus stared at it for a moment, unable to speak.

Plutarius was watching him closely. "How did I get it? I'm the Chief Centurion, a powerful and influential position. You told me you had personal business in Rome, so I thought you might have written there about it. I ordered the mail bags from your century to be brought to me and I searched through them till I found this." He tapped his fingernail on the tablet. "Calvinia is a lovely name. And she works in a shop, just as I predicted."

"Chief Centurion, I must insist on—"

"You can insist on nothing!" Plutarius' voice quickly sharpened. "The army is your life, Glaxus. You must realize that. The empire needs you more than the disgraced daughter of a disgraced senator. I've heard of what Andorus brought upon his house. This woman would be better off if she were dead."

Glaxus clenched his fists as he struggled to keep his temper. "You can stop the letter, sir, but you can't stop me. When my enlistment is up, not even the Emperor can extend it against my will. I'll then go directly to Calvinia in Rome. I will not be your successor."

Sighing deeply, Plutarius put the tablet into Glaxus' hands. Glaxus immediately opened it and saw that the wax was blank. He then examined the exterior more closely. It wasn't the same one he'd gotten from Pindocles. This was made of darker wood and had no address on it. He gave Plutarius a startled look.

"I returned your letter to the bag after reading it. It's going to Rome with the others. The mail detachment left about three hours ago." Plutarius reached up and squeezed Glaxus' shoulder. "I thought perhaps one last attempt might change your mind, but in case that didn't happen, I let the letter go. I hope you find happiness with her."

Unsure how to respond, Glaxus chose not to, and slipped the tablet into a pocket in his cloak. He stood silently beside Plutarius, feeling an odd blend of anger, relief, and respect.

When the pyre was ready for Fabius' cremation, all available centuries from the 19th Legion were called to the assembly ground. The 19th's five remaining tribunes were also there. Glaxus listened in disgust as they argued openly over which of them would lead the next bear hunt. They ignored the body of their peer as six cavalry officers carried it from the infirmary.

After the corpse was in place, Tridonis walked alone out of the headquarters building and stood beside the platform. At his appearance, even the tribunes were quiet. A moment later, Varus left headquarters and began strutting toward the pyre. Glaxus thought it odd that they didn't come out together.

Unlike Tridonis, the General was followed by a group of civilians. They were probably scribes, assistants, and various other sycophants. Varus himself appeared to be somewhere between fifty-five and sixty. Though about the same age as Plutarius, his physical condition was clearly inferior to that of the Chief Centurion. His elaborate breastplate was strapped on loosely to accommodate his bulging stomach while his helmet appeared uncomfortably small. Glaxus could see Calvinia was right. This man was obviously not a real soldier and never had been.

As the General approached, he gestured to his entourage to stay back a few steps. He walked past Tridonis without a glance and heaved himself up the stairs of the platform. In a voice obviously practiced in public oratory, he spoke of Fabius as a "courageous young patrician whose valor, selflessness, and sense of duty were an example to all Romans." There was more, but beyond that Glaxus found it hard to pay serious attention.

Varus finished speaking, then asked for a torch and held it to the pyre. While the flames had seemed reluctant to take Quintar, they roared through the corpse of Fabius. The General had to quickly stumble down the stairs to keep from being singed. "By my father's ghost!" he exclaimed. "The body burns like Avernus!"

When the ashes had been gathered and the troops dismissed, one of Varus' assistants approached Plutarius and Glaxus.

"The General and the Legate want to see you immediately, Chief Centurion. Senior Centurion Glaxus is also ordered to report."

Varus and Tridonis were standing by the platform and Plutarius instantly began walking toward them. Glaxus hesitated before going along. Though commonplace for a Chief Centurion, such a meeting was rare for those of lesser rank. Plutarius had said the Legate would personally commend him for his training of Herman. That had to be it.

As they drew near, the General spoke first. His manner was blunt and direct. "Plutarius, I am still not pleased with the speed of preparations for the campaign. I wish to begin marching east very soon. After sundown today we will confer again on how best to accelerate our plans. Agreed?"

Glaxus didn't like the sound of this, but since his opinion wasn't asked, he knew it shouldn't be offered. Bypassing the chain of command was always dangerous. Doing so in the General's presence would be insane.

Though once asked, an honest appraisal was always expected. Plutarius did not fall short in that regard. "No sir, I do not agree. My counsel is as it was. Readiness is paramount and need not be rushed. As I said earlier, I recommend a few months of training and scouting. Commander Herman was only dispatched this morning. Leaving before we hear from him would be unwise in my judgment."

Glaxus recalled his conversation with Herman at dawn during preparations for the bear hunt. So that's why the new commander was at headquarters so early. He was there to be briefed before being sent on a scouting patrol across the Rhine.

General Varus listened to the Chief Centurion with obvious impatience. "I believe we know all we need to. I also believe we are ready to defeat the stupid barbarians right now if they abandon the alliance. It's possible to be too cautious. Indeed, overestimating one's opponent can be fatal. Tonight, we will draw up final plans for deployment and marching sequence. We leave within two weeks. A priest of Mars has accompanied me from Rome and I have no doubt his omen will be propitious." Varus squinted at Glaxus. "Tridonis, is this the Senior Centurion of whom Herman spoke so highly?"

"Yes sir." Tridonis gripped forearms with Glaxus. "Well done, Centurion. And not for the first time, either. I have heard your name mentioned with respect throughout the legion." Glaxus then saw the Legate glance at Plutarius, who shook his head very slightly. Tridonis frowned. "Best wishes in civilian life."

"Thank you, sir." Glaxus shifted his eyes back to Plutarius, who looked away.

"Civilian life?" said Varus. "You are retiring after this campaign?"

Being directly spoken to by the General was unnerving, but Glaxus was calm enough to realize his responses had best be brief. "Yes sir."

"You have no ambition beyond the rank of Senior Centurion?"
"No sir."
"Where were you born?"
"Rome, sir."
"You will retire there?"
"Yes sir."
"Your family's cognomen and your father's occupation?"

"Our cognomen is Valtinius, sir, and my father was a senatorial assistant of the second rank. He's dead now."

"What senators did he serve?"

"At the time of his death, sir, he was in the service of Senator Andorus."

"Ah, yes. Andorus. I knew him before the shame of expulsion befell him. He's dead as well." The General tapped his ill-fitting helmet. "As I recall, Andorus had a most attractive daughter, a raven-haired beauty. I can't think of her name just now, but that old dog Hyboreas had picked her to marry as his next prize. He goes through one or two a year. This one's a fine piece of meat, I can tell you. I wonder if Hyboreas caught her. Do you know the woman I mean, Centurion? Perhaps your father mentioned her."

Glaxus understood that self-restraint now was paramount. An angry reply to the General could cost him his retirement pension, his future with Calvinia, even his head. He was simply going to say "No sir" and hope for an end to the questions, but Plutarius spoke first.

"May I suggest we let Centurion Glaxus get some rest, sir? The bear hunt this morning has surely left him tired."

"Yes, I've heard of his heroics, and I've been told he held the sword for Fabius as well." Varus leaned closer to Glaxus. "But the cavalry officers also inform me that you did so reluctantly, and that you tried very hard to dissuade him from suicide. Is this true?"

Glaxus cursed his luck. Plutarius had guided him out of one snare and into another. "Yes sir, it's true."

"By all the gods! What for? He eagerly sought that assignment from me. When he failed, was it not his duty to kill himself?"

Glaxus tried to choose his words carefully. "The Tribune felt it was, sir, and he did so. I only suggested that he could find a means outside the army to serve the empire. It seemed such a waste of ability."

This response surprised Varus. "That's not a very Roman attitude, Centurion."

"Rome is indeed a military society," Tridonis interposed, "and success in civilian life usually follows only after success in the army. However, I don't see why it need be so. Surely the General would agree that not everyone is suited to be a soldier."

It was plain to Glaxus these words were meant not only to rescue him, but also to make Varus wince. That they did. The General tugged self-consciously on his breastplate as he kept his eyes down. "Yes, well, I think our business here is concluded. We'll meet again an hour after sundown."

Plutarius and the Legate both nodded at Varus as he led his entourage back to headquarters.

Holding back a sigh of relief, Glaxus turned to Plutarius. "Permission to withdraw, sir?"

It was Tridonis who answered. "Permission granted, Centurion. And henceforward, I suggest you keep your unroman thoughts between your ears and away from your tongue, at least until you're out of the army. Do I make myself clear?"

"You do, sir."

"Then you're dismissed."

As Glaxus turned to go, Plutarius winked at him and grinned.

He rejoined his century at the small lake near the fort's north side. Before attending the cremations, he'd spent the early afternoon with his men digging the sanitation holes. Now they had just completed wrestling drills under the supervision of Likas, the new optio.

Likas had been the century's signifer and was therefore next in line for advancement behind Macro. He was not as ebullient as Macro, but had demonstrated a cool head in battle, bearing aloft the century's standard while fighting raged around him. He had also proven himself trustworthy in his other duty of operating the century's savings bank. Plutarius agreed with Glaxus that he deserved this opportunity and he was therefore promoted.

The men were by the lake's edge, stripping off their tunics. Likas met Glaxus as he approached.

"The wrestling went well, Optio?"

"Yes sir."

Glaxus looked him over and saw his knees were dirty. "You participated?"

"Yes sir."

"Well done. Swimming is next?"

"It is, sir, and we have two auxiliaries in a log boat in case someone gets into trouble. Will you lead?"

"You will, but I'll join in." Glaxus turned around so Likas could help him off with his armor. "Is the water cold?"

"Yes sir, but not intolerable."

"Good. It'll make the men tough." Glaxus noticed the sun was very low and wondered whether Macro was still at the infirmary. He asked Likas if there had been any word.

"Yes sir. He was taken back to the barracks with orders to rest."

"Very well. I'll see him later." When everyone was naked, Glaxus waded into the water. "The Optio will lead you to the far shore and back. Begin."

Though the lake was cool, its surface was smooth and fit for swimming. Keeping the century in front of him, Glaxus frog kicked with his head up, looking for anyone who might get a cramp or become tired. The two Germanic Gauls in the boat glided along beside him, their oars nearly silent. When a soldier stopped swimming and began treading water, they paddled over without waiting for an order from Glaxus. After they asked in broken Latin if he was all right, the soldier nodded, but grabbed the side of the boat to rest a minute before continuing.

Watching Gauls help a Roman, Glaxus suddenly thought of Herman. Was he having any luck on his reconnaissance patrol? And was he really scouting for the Romans? Perhaps he and others were up to something else on the east side of the Rhine.

Glaxus dipped his face in the water and shook his head. Such suspicions were a waste of time for a centurion. It was Varus who needed to consider such things.

The soldier released his grip on the boat and continued. When the swim was completed, Glaxus thanked the auxiliaries for their attention to duty.

"It was nothing, sir," said one, laboring through the Latin pronunciation. "Our comrade just needed a little help."

"Well done nonetheless. Now return to your commanding officer." Glaxus watched them walk away and asked himself if his thoughts in the water had been fair.

Upon returning to the barracks, Glaxus told Likas to have the men put their armor away and march to the evening meal in their tunics. Inside, he found Macro lying with his head propped up on a folded blanket.

"Come in, Glaxus. Likas said you had swimming drill today."

"Yes." Glaxus hung his ring mail on its peg. "And the water was colder than it has been. Autumn must be coming on."

"Better not let your balls freeze," laughed Macro. "You'll need them when you retire in Rome." His left arm and shoulder were heavily wrapped in linen. The same material was wound about his head, covering his left eye. On the table between the cots were a cup of red wine and a small metal box.

Glaxus sat on his mattress and looked at his friend. He had told himself Macro's injuries and Quintar's death were a result of ambition and primarily their own doing. Now he didn't feel so certain. He suddenly heard himself saying, "I'm sorry, Macro."

"Bah! It wasn't your fault!"

"Wasn't it? I knew Fabius was trouble as soon he walked in here."

"But what could you do about it? Orders are to be obeyed."

"A javelin in his back would have solved everything. I could've said there was thick fog in the forest and I thought he was a Gaul."

"You'd never have done that. You're a soldier, not a murderer. Besides, Varus wouldn't have believed you. You'd have been executed immediately. Come now, Glaxus. The truth is we brought it on ourselves. Quintar, Fabius, and me. Now we've paid for it. Actually, I got off the lightest. I'm still alive." Macro shook some white powder from the small box into the wine. "The good physician gave me this for the pain. I was afraid to ask what it is." He sipped from the cup and grimaced. "That reminds me. Did Fabius burn well?"

"Yes, I'm glad to say. Quintar's pyre had to be reignited, but Nemesis must have wanted to get her hands on Fabius. He went up like . . . like . . ."

"Like he was full of olive oil?"

Glaxus was stunned into silence for a moment, then it dawned on him. "Pindocles!"

"Yes," said Macro. "After patching me up, he let me watch as he dissected Fabius. He said he'd heard that Varus would light the Tribune's pyre and he wanted to give the General a surprise. So after finishing his examination, he removed the internal organs and filled the body with olive oil."

"Then the Greek has a sense of humor after all. And that fool Varus nearly killed himself tripping down the stairs to escape the flames. If he had, Tridonis would have been left in command and the campaign wouldn't begin until we were ready."

"When it begins is of no matter to me anymore. I'm off to Rome tomorrow. My discharge will be completed when I get there."

"Then what?" asked Glaxus.

"One of my uncles has a business loading and unloading ships in Ostia. He's often told me I can join in with him whenever I leave the army. Now's the time, it would seem. And since Ostia is only some twenty-five miles down the Tiber from Rome, you must come see me when you retire."

"Of course I will, if I live to retire."

"And why wouldn't you? You've survived tougher campaigns than this is likely to be. Since the alliance is holding west of the Rhine, it'll surely have some effect on the east side as well. If the Gauls over there know what's good for them, they'll accept Rome and become one of our client states. You shouldn't expect more than a few skirmishes."

"I hope you're right, but I wish Varus would let us properly prepare just the same."

Macro took another swallow of wine. "He's the General. His word is law and there's nothing you can do about it."

They talked a while longer, with Macro boasting of his uncle's business and how he'd rather be rich than a Praetorian anyway. When his eyelids began to droop, Glaxus eased the cup from his hand and pulled a blanket over him.

Standing there for a moment, Glaxus wished it were possible to take Macro's injuries upon himself and be the one going home tomorrow. Now that he was committed to Calvinia, he wanted to see her more than ever. Why did he have to stay here with that idiot Varus? Why couldn't Augustus just be satisfied with the size of the empire? Why didn't—

But such thinking was unsoldierly. "Just do your duty," he whispered. "If you die, so be it. She's strong. She'll survive."

He put out the lamp and got into his cot. In the dark, he was surprised to hear Macro mutter, "If the gods are kind, you'll be with her again. I can take her a message when I get to Rome if you like, in case your letter doesn't reach her. Now stop talking to yourself and let me get some sleep."

"You're a good friend, Macro."

"Yes. Good night."

At sunrise, Glaxus got up to write another copy of his letter. Not wanting to bother Pindocles again, he was about to settle for birchbark. He then remembered he had in his cloak the blank wax tablet with which Plutarius tried to bluff him. He wasn't prepared to say it was fate, though he thought it odd how things sometimes happened.

He remembered exactly what he had written and used a nail to quickly put it down in the wax. After addressing the outside of the tablet, Glaxus awakened Macro and helped him prepare to travel. When ready to go, Macro took the letter and slipped it into his tunic.

"I'll get it to her."

"I know you will."

They clasped forearms at the barracks door, then Macro walked over to headquarters. Varus was sending another detachment to Rome with more pre-campaign reports for the Emperor. He'd been doing so daily since his arrival. The fact that it would take weeks for each report to get there didn't seem to bother him. Glaxus thought it a waste of manpower, but knew Macro was glad to go along with the next detachment and get home that much sooner.

The next seven days passed quickly as preparations for the campaign continued. During that time, a second expedition was sent after bears under the command of a tribune named Cornelius. To Glaxus' relief, he was not ordered to go along, but he happened to be at headquarters when the expedition returned. It had not failed. The baying hounds couldn't drown out the furious bawling of the captive bears. The huge beasts rocked their crates from side to side as the wagons rolled to a stop.

Cornelius was elated. "Three big males!" he crowed, leaping from his horse. "And no one hurt or killed! We netted them first, then got ropes around their paws and over their snouts. All praise to the divine Diana! I must sacrifice in her honor tonight for the glorious success she has brought me!"

Glaxus thought it best to scoff at this in silence. No goddess of hunting was involved. Cornelius prevailed by doing the right things in the right order. He'd brought along the same cavalry officers that accompanied Fabius. They undoubtedly counseled him against repeating his predecessor's blunders. Now a selfish young man would see his worth rise in the eyes of Varus and the Emperor. Meanwhile, the bears were destined to slaughter and be slaughtered for the enjoyment of cheering crowds. Glaxus didn't believe such results could truly be called success.

But Cornelius clearly thought so. He and his friends engaged in drunken revels that night, sacrificing a pig in Diana's honor and pouring out libations to her. The stone building where the tribunes lived was ringing with laughter when Plutarius and Glaxus walked by. They passed the entrance in time to see a dozen women from the traveling brothels climbing off a wagon. The tribunes and cavalry officers came out to carry them in, shouting the vulgar details of what would happen next.

Glaxus turned away. "It's as though their friend never existed, they forget him so quickly."

"As Fabius would have forgotten any of them," said Plutarius. "Among such men friendship is only a tool to be used. Each lives for himself alone. May Pluto take them all! Come on."

The Chief Centurion had said nothing about the planning session Varus called for on the day of the cremations. This made Glaxus guess that Plutarius and Tridonis had once again asked the General for more time and were once again denied.

Tonight Plutarius had ordered Glaxus to join him for a walk through the fort and surrounding encampments. There were now some thirty thousand people prepared to cross the Rhine and establish the new colony, twenty thousand soldiers and ten thousand non-combatants.

The entire civilian area swarmed with activity, like a city. Light from hundreds of campfires and oil lamps made walking easy. Children recognized Plutarius' rank and saluted as he and Glaxus passed their tents. The babble of voices was everywhere and the evening breeze had become thick with the smell of cooking. Glaxus was reminded of growing up in Rome's Aventine district.

Every one of these people had to be moved across the Rhine and established in possibly hostile territory. The reality of this task suddenly came to Glaxus while looking out across the encampment. Did Emperor Augustus really understand what he was telling them to do? And who was this old man who gave such orders, directing their lives with his merest wish? Like most Romans, Glaxus had never laid eyes on him. Having rescued the empire from the chaos of civil war after Caesar's murder, he was virtually deified, his person being declared sacrosanct by the senate. Augustus claimed that Rome was still a republic, but there was no doubt anywhere he was the real and sole power in the empire. And as long as order and prosperity were maintained, few Romans complained. Glaxus certainly never did before now.

He and Plutarius had begun walking along the encampment's outer perimeter when a detail of soldiers carrying torches approached from straight ahead. "Chief Centurion!"

Plutarius waved them forward. "Here."

"Sir, we have been sent by the Legate to find you. You must join him and the General in war council immediately. A message has been received from Commander Herman."

Plutarius gazed at the ground for a moment before speaking to Glaxus. "Accompany me."

"To a war council, sir?"

"Yes."

This was highly unusual and likely to be resisted, especially by Varus. After all, Glaxus was only a Senior Centurion. If he was under consideration for Chief Centurion it would make sense, but he had told the General face to face he wasn't interested in being promoted. What was Plutarius up to now?

"Sir, one of my rank doesn't attend—"

"One of your rank attends where one of my rank orders him to attend." Plutarius barked at the soldiers. "I'm on my way! Return to your duties!"

As the detail left, Plutarius began striding toward the fort, Glaxus pacing uneasily at his side.

"Calm down, Glaxus. I'm not trying again to trap you into taking my place. Having trained Herman, you know him best. Your advice in interpreting his message could be useful. You will wait outside while I suggest this to the General, then we'll see. Understood?"

"Yes sir." Glaxus was relieved and worried at the same time. This wasn't another ruse, but he still might find himself in a war council. That was somewhere he had never been and never expected to be, especially after turning down the promotion. If the General permitted him to enter, how would the others receive him? He didn't think Tridonis would mind, but what of the tribunes? Perhaps he'd be lucky and Varus would say no. Besides, he considered it unlikely he could be of any real help.

Moments later he was standing down the hall from the council room after Plutarius had gone in. When he heard the door opening again, he hoped to see the Chief Centurion coming to tell him he was dismissed.

It was Cornelius, trudging wearily down the hall. His bloodshot eyes clearly revealed he'd been in the middle of his carousals when called away. The resentment he felt at Glaxus' presence was no less evident.

"Ah! Trainer of Herman, slayer of bears, sword-holder for tribunes. The only man in living memory to turn down the rank of Chief Centurion. How good of you to honor us with this visitation." He jabbed his thumb toward the door. "Get in there!"

Glaxus hated cowards who hid behind their rank, but knew that was common in the military and would never change. He made no reply to Cornelius. Looking toward the council room, he took a deep breath and started forward.

V

Cornelius entered behind him and pulled the door shut. The room was as Glaxus imagined it, austere and functional. Oil lamps hung from the low ceiling over a large table bearing tablets and sheepskin maps. The General was seated at the table with the Legate. Plutarius was to the right, standing behind Tridonis. On the room's opposite side, Cornelius joined the other tribunes as they leaned against the stone wall. With sneering faces and folded arms, they watched Glaxus approach the General and salute.

"Senior Centurion Glaxus Claudius Valtinius, sir, reporting as ordered."

Steadily drumming his fingers on the table, Varus glanced at the Legate and grunted. Tridonis then addressed Glaxus while holding out a roll of birchbark.

"The Chief Centurion has suggested you may be of assistance concerning this communication the General received from Commander Herman. It was relayed to us by a system of Gaulish couriers. Read the message aloud, study the map, and tell us what you think."

"But be quick about it!" snapped Cornelius.

Glaxus was not surprised when this remark went unrebuked by Varus, though Tridonis cast a cold glance at the tribunes. Yet Cornelius was right. He had better read it, briefly give his opinion, and get out. He took the bark and unrolled it. The message was in rather formal Latin.

"General Varus—All things bode well for your expedition across the Rhine. You may proceed immediately. The Cherusci on this side are eager to become a Roman client state. There is opposition among some of the lesser tribes, but nothing you can't easily suppress. As long as the Emperor lets the people maintain their ancient customs, most of them see no reason to refuse the protection of his legions. Here is a map of the route I suggest. I will await you east of the Teutoburg Hills and we can then discuss the most suitable places to put settlements. May the blessings of best and greatest Jupiter be upon you."

It sounded very Roman. More so than Herman seemed on the morning of the bear hunt. As for the map, Glaxus wasn't sure what to make of it. The indicated route went across the Rhine and east up the valley of the Lippe River. Twenty years earlier the Roman General Drusus Germanicus had built a series of forts along the Lippe, all of which were still manned. Plutarius and Tridonis regularly made visits to these outposts. That part of the march would be in familiar territory.

The route then turned sharply off the Lippe at Fort Aliso and headed north, presumably into the heart of Cherusci tribal lands. Roman knowledge of that area was limited. Glaxus had heard Gauls in the auxiliary units talk of marshes to the northeast, but he saw none on the map. It did indicate hills as the message said.

"Well, Centurion?" Varus was still drumming his fingers.

"It sounds promising, sir." Glaxus set the message on the table. "But I would recommend the route be thoroughly scouted before we put our main body of troops on it."

"That's what I sent Herman to do and he has done it."

"Yes sir, but I would suggest it be double-checked."

Varus shook his head. "That would cost too much time. The way has been chosen by someone who was born and raised there and knows the land well. We will set out on this route shortly. You're dismissed."

Those last two words were what Glaxus most wanted to hear, but now that he had, he hesitated. "Sir, may I ask if Segestes' current whereabouts are known?"

Cornelius stepped away from the wall. "The General has dismissed you!"

Tridonis spoke softly but firmly. "The General doesn't need you to second his orders, Tribune. Remain silent and keep your place." He then looked at Glaxus. "You refer to the father-in-law of Herman, correct?"

Varus was clearly unhappy at seeing the Legate assert himself, but couldn't very well censure the second-in-command in front of the Tribunes and Chief Centurion. Recognizing this, Glaxus kept his eyes off Varus and on Tridonis.

"Yes sir. That's correct. I met him when he came to the fort for the first meeting about the alliance. If I may make a recommendation, we should find him and ask him to . . . to enlighten us concerning this message and the route on the map."

"Enlighten us?" Tridonis raised an eyebrow. "Don't mince words, Centurion. You think we should determine if Herman is lying in this message."

"Yes sir. There would be no harm in confirming its accuracy. The delay would be acceptable in my opinion."

"Not in mine." Varus shifted his bulk around in his chair and spoke with obvious irritation. "The Emperor watches us closely, Centurion. He watches the north and waits. If we tarry, he will not be pleased."

"Nevertheless," said Tridonis, "I agree that consulting Segestes would be a wise precaution and well worth the few days it would take. He's several miles to the south of us, sir, in the region where the Erft flows into the Rhine. He told us he was going to make sure the alliance was holding among his clans there. We could send a cavalry detachment to find him."

Shifting and grunting once again, Varus seemed about to reply when Cornelius did it for him. "With most sincere respect to the Legate, the General is right. We cannot afford the time. What if Segestes is no longer at the junction of the Erft and the Rhine? We could be weeks tracking him down."

Glaxus realized this might well be true, but was certain that conferring with Segestes should be done no matter how long it delayed the campaign. The chieftain had seemed a straightforward man who wouldn't give his word lightly. If he was down by the Erft checking on the alliance among his clansmen, then he likely believed in it and was committed to making it work.

Plutarius spoke up. "Sir, any time spent in finding Segestes would give us a chance to hone our preparations still further. The General knows that I think we are in too much of a hurry."

"I have three legions at my command," Varus replied. "Whatever opposition we encounter cannot possibly stop us and will be crushed without mercy. If the Gauls break the alliance, whole villages will be wiped out as a lesson to them. Their children will also be killed to break their morale." He tapped the message. "It would be good if Herman speaks truly here and the Gauls are ready to welcome us, but either way, the Emperor shall be obeyed. As the poet Ovid tells us, the end justifies the means."

"Indeed?" said Tridonis. "Would that be the same Ovid who used his poetry as a means of insulting the Emperor, with the end result being that Augustus felt justified in banishing him to the Moesia Province last year?"

Glaxus saw Plutarius stifle a smile while Varus and the Tribunes glared at the Legate.

"We march a week from today," announced the General, "and that's final. Besides the new pontoon bridge, the river fleet is sending triremes to ferry some of our people up the Lippe. I'll have a garrison of troops stay behind to maintain this fort." He looked sternly at Glaxus. "We'll not waste time finding Segestes and we won't doubt the veracity of Commander Herman. The Emperor has chosen him over Segestes to be the Gaul's spokesman. Also, he shall eventually succeed his father-in-law as supreme chief of the Cherusci, so it is with him we should deal. Whether he's being honest or not is ultimately academic. Such is the will of Augustus, such is the will of the Senate and People of Rome." Varus stood up. As Tridonis tried to do the same, the General put a meaty hand on his shoulder and held him down. "Do you all understand?"

"Yes sir!" blurted the Tribunes in unison.

For Plutarius, the words obviously didn't come with ease. "Understood, sir."

Knowing it was his turn, Glaxus spoke as quietly as he could while still being heard. "Yes sir."

Tridonis slipped his shoulder from under Varus' hand and got to his feet. "We understand, General, but not all of us agree with you. Killing children is not why we joined the—"

"Enough! I have made my decision!" Varus gestured to Cornelius and his companions. "I will continue this council with the tribunes. Thank you for your suggestions, Tridonis. You and the Chief Centurion may go. Take the Senior Centurion with you."

Plutarius emitted a gasp. Even Cornelius seemed shocked. Varus wanted to conduct war council with junior officers while dismissing his second-in-command. Glaxus couldn't imagine Tridonis would swallow this.

And he didn't. "If the General's opinion is that I'm not fit to attend war council, than neither can I be fit to remain in the Emperor's army. I would have to immediately retire to Rome, and if his Imperial Majesty wishes, I will explain to him how you found me inadequate to remain in his service."

Glaxus thought this a brilliant and courageous move. Augustus' would surely want to know why his handpicked choice to lead the 19th Legion was retiring just before a major campaign. When the Legate told him, it would then be Varus' turn to explain. And everyone in the room knew Tridonis wasn't bluffing.

The General suddenly and visibly lost his nerve. Loudly clearing his throat, he shuffled through the maps on the table for a moment before waving his hand at the door. "Perhaps there is no need to continue the council, after all. The decision to march has been made, so we can adjourn. Everyone is dismissed." He glanced at the tribunes. "Everyone."

Being the lowest ranking officer there, Glaxus knew he should get out of the General's presence first. He was through the door and halfway down the hall when Plutarius overtook him.

"Come, Glaxus. Onto the assembly ground."

Once outside, Glaxus inhaled a lungful of night air and tried to let the tension flow out of him. "A most enjoyable experience, Chief Centurion. Thank you so much."

"Now you know what the Legate and I have had to put up with ever since that jackass took command. A worse combination of stupidity and arrogance I've never seen. All we can do is hope that if Herman is planning something traitorous, we will have sufficient force to overcome him and any allies he may have."

"The General offers us no other option."

Plutarius nodded, then fell silent as they walked.

Glaxus began thinking over what Varus had said. He understood the General's intention to succeed through sheer might and ruthlessness. It was often a military necessity. Glaxus hadn't forgotten that after his century was ambushed, he ordered Macro to hang the dead chieftain's head from a tree as he'd seen done with Roman heads.

But he had killed the chieftain fairly during battle. In nearly twenty years of service he hadn't once harmed women, children, or prisoners of war. He wondered if that was only because he'd never been ordered to.

Also, if the alliance fell apart and full-scale hostilities began, Gaulish warriors would certainly seize any opportunity to kill Roman children. Many officers and legionaries would therefore agree with Varus that a similar policy of brutality would be required in response. Glaxus had heard of such tactics being used by the Roman army in the past, as when Carthage was razed 155 years ago. If they were used again, Augustus probably wouldn't care to know about it as long as military objectives were met.

But Glaxus now asked himself bluntly if this was an order he could obey. He envisioned himself with sword in hand, standing over a Gaulish infant.

"Chief Centurion, I must concur with the Legate. Killing children is not why I joined the army. If ordered to do so, I will refuse, as I know you will."

"Yes, and others will refuse also, but there are many who would gladly do it, especially if Varus lets word spread among the troops of his willingness to look down and not up. The fat coward is more apt to use that method instead of directly ordering it. He could thus evade responsibility should the Emperor disapprove, which would be unlikely. If it happens, Glaxus, you and I won't be able to stop it, but at least our hands will be clean of innocent blood."

Glaxus couldn't deny any of this. The Roman army, including his own century, was not largely made up of humanitarians. What army was or ever would be? Although required to read and write as a qualification for enlisting, recruits were not expected to be deep thinkers. In fact, such a quality was considered detrimental in soldiers. They were expected to do as they were told and leave the thinking to their superiors, an attitude most of them willingly embraced. Glaxus himself was the same way as a young legionary.

But then he grew older, advanced through the ranks, and met Calvinia. She would certainly prefer he died an honorable death on the battlefield rather than survive by killing children.

When they reached the barracks area, Plutarius placed a hand on Glaxus' arm. "In the end, these things lie in the lap of the gods. Let us choose as wisely as we can, and trust them to guide events to the right conclusion. Good night, my friend."

"Good night, sir."

A week later Varus awakened at midnight to consult the omen. The Tribunes attended eagerly, the Legate and Chief Centurion because they were ordered to. Glaxus was not disappointed to be left out. As Plutarius told him a few hours later, the priest of Mars sprinkled grain on the floor of the council room. A small cage was then opened, releasing two chickens that had been hatched and raised in Mars' temple at Rome. If the birds ate the grain, the omen for the campaign would be favorable. If they consumed little or none, the omen would be bad and the start of the campaign would be in jeopardy. They had promptly devoured all the grain, so Varus and the priest declared it a good time to begin marching.

Glaxus reminded Plutarius that at Fabius' cremation Varus said the omen was sure to be propitious. "So were I that priest, I'd know what was good for me and what wasn't. I'd starve the damn birds for a day and a night before using them for the omen. They'd be certain to gobble up the grain, the General would be pleased, and the campaign could begin."

Plutarius laughed and said he didn't doubt it. "But you'd be wise to remember the Legate's advice, Glaxus, and keep those suspicions behind your teeth."

The march began that day at dawn. Fort Vetera was only three miles from the intersection of the Rhine and the Lippe. Glaxus was sure that's why it was picked as the starting point for the campaign. From here, communications with the Rhine flotilla would be easy and fast. On hills near the river were watchtowers with huge stacks of wood ready to be burned as signal fires. There were similar stations on hills throughout Rome's Gaulish provinces. Glaxus and his century once spent a week on such duty, manning a tower halfway between the river and the fort.

He was mustering his men on the assembly ground when the guards on the parapets began shouting, "Signal fire! Signal fire!" This meant the flotilla was in position near the junction of the rivers and ready to begin ferry operations. After a quick march to the riverbank, Glaxus learned from the embarkation officer that his century would be among those going to Fort Aliso on foot. This was fine with him. He had traveled by ship before and it always made him queasy.

The pontoon bridge had only been completed the previous day. The pounding of hobnail sandals on the planks combined loudly with horses' hooves and the clattering of wheels. Glaxus had to shout directions to his men as they crossed, centuries to the right, wagons and cavalry units to the left.

At the pier next to the bridge he saw a small number of soldiers and civilians being separately loaded onto triremes. Children crowded into the bows, pointing ahead excitedly. The ships were to row up the Lippe to Fort Aliso where they'd be met by the main column coming overland.

But how was it decided who would be spared a long portion of foot-travel? There was probably some low-level bribing involved, most likely among ship commanders. This sort of thing was openly accepted in the Roman military. Glaxus had frequently been offered money by legionaries in exchange for excusing them from work details. He always resisted the temptation. Never having bought indulgence as a young soldier, he wouldn't sell it now.

When his century was halfway across, Glaxus was surprised to see Pindocles bumping along the bridge on a wagon. He'd have thought someone so highly regarded by Tridonis would be among that privileged group being rowed up the Lippe. The physician's wagon was loaded with his medical supplies and driven by one of the Legate's slaves. Glaxus trotted over to it as it rattled past.

"Greetings, healing master! You grace us with your presence! Was there no ship befitting your magnificence?"

Pindocles aimed his sharp nose at Glaxus and scowled. "The Centurion's jaw opens most freely. Perhaps it will be broken in battle one day and I shall have an opportunity to sew it shut."

"Perhaps," laughed Glaxus. "But I'm sure you'd rather have a chance to cut me open and fill me with olive oil."

The doctor smiled faintly. "A man of your stature would contain enough to make a most explosive display."

"Yes. Between the two of us we might get old Varus next time, although you'll excuse me if I'd rather finish my last year alive and retire in Rome." Glaxus noticed something about Pindocles' face. "You seem pale, Greek. Are you unwell?"

"Crossing bridges has always been difficult for me. It's more a condition of the reason than the body, though the body feels its effects."

Glaxus hadn't expected such a blunt admission of infirmity from Pindocles. "I think I understand. I dislike traveling by ship. I can deal with it if I must, but it makes my stomach weak. Will you recover when you're off the bridge?"

"Yes. I'm here only because it was decided one physician should travel by land to Fort Aliso in case anyone was sick or injured en route."

"And you nobly volunteered?"

"I most certainly did not. Varus brought several Egyptian physicians with him and the scoundrels conspired to shut me out of their company. They finally managed to have me assigned here."

"The Legate couldn't help you?"

"He tried, but the Egyptians convinced Varus that since I was the most experienced at dealing with wounds, I should travel with the troops. The jackals just wanted to be rid of me because they resent my superior ability. They fear that if Varus were to become ill, none but I could cure him and they would fall out of his favor."

This didn't surprise Glaxus. If ambition and envy motivated soldiers, why not doctors? He tapped Pindocles' arm with his vinestick. "Listen, Greek. The sons of Pharaoh may be right in spite of their intentions. Are you not the best? We're glad to have you among us. If my rooster gets chopped off in battle, I wouldn't trust anyone but you to sew it on straight. And if the General dies under the Egyptians' care, their pickled heads will be sent to their mothers and Tridonis will assume command. May the gods grant us that!"

Pindocles found this humorous and began to laugh. Glaxus realized he'd never heard the physician do so before. The rapid, high-pitched cackle made his hair stand up under his helmet.

"May they grant that indeed, my fr-" Then the Greek recovered his cold demeanor as swiftly as he lost it. "And may the gods also grant that you never become available for olive oil duty. Now perhaps you should return to your troops, Centurion. Without your directions the imbeciles could march into the river."

Glaxus stepped away from the wagon as it continued along the bridge. Pindocles had begun to call him friend, then stopped. He didn't know whether to be insulted or relieved.

The march up the Lippe valley to Fort Aliso took two days and was without incident. The road constructed by General Drusus twenty years earlier had been well maintained. Those who had come by ship were already encamped in and around the fort.

Glaxus arrived with his century in the late afternoon. A decurion with a detail of ten men was meeting incoming troops and leading them to campsites. Because Glaxus was a senior centurion, he could stay in a barracks inside the fort and decided to do so. He believed in living and working with his men and had camped in tents with them the last two nights. Still, he knew he had to use the privileges of his rank on occasion or their regard for him would slip. Though before entering the fort, he went with the century to the campsite. Likas was a new optio and would probably appreciate a little advice.

The site was near the river. Many centuries were already encamped while others were still involved in the process. As the tents were removed from the wagons and unfolded, Glaxus took Likas aside. "After camp is established, get the men to the cookhouse and see that they're not shorted on food. Don't be shy about standing up for their needs. Fight for them off the battlefield and they'll fight for you on it."

"I will, sir."

"Make sure they get some sleep, but ask around first to see if anyone sustained an injury during the march, such as a twisted ankle. Sometimes they're too proud to tell you. When I was a nineteen year-old legionary, I once marched eleven miles on a sore knee to prove my manhood. I only proved myself a fool."

"I'll ask around, sir."

"And one more thing." Glaxus offered Likas the vinestick. "If anyone gives you trouble, you must not be afraid to thump him. You're a bit on the quiet side and they will see how far they can push you. A couple of hard blows above the waist on the first one to get insolent should make your attitude clear. Don't enjoy it, but by all the gods, don't let them think you lack the belly for it. The difference between respect and fear must be kept small. Do you hear my words, Optio?"

Likas gripped the vinestick tightly. "I hear you, Centurion." Then his lean face eased into a slight grin. "You used this on me once, sir."

Glaxus couldn't remember, but didn't doubt it. "When?"

"Nearly a year ago when we were on a training march. I was retying my helmet cord and didn't mind where I was stepping. As I wandered a few paces out of formation, you jabbed me in the ribs and told me to return to my place."

"Yes, now I recall. I also recall you getting back in formation with great speed, and once you had, I didn't strike you again. Correct?"

"Yes sir."

"Well, the wheel has turned for you. But never forget that power brings responsibility."

"I won't, Centurion."

Glaxus knew there was nothing to do next but leave things in his optio's hands. "I'll return tomorrow at dawn. Have the men in their armor upon my arrival and ready to assume marching formation."

"Yes sir."

Once inside the fort's main gate, Glaxus found the assembly ground swarming with soldiers and civilians. He picked his way across to a row of barracks on the far side and met the junior centurion in charge of billeting.

"Name, sir?"

"Senior Centurion Glaxus, 19th Legion."

The young man peered at his wax tablets. "You're in barracks three, sir, bed seven. I also have a notation near your name saying you are to report to headquarters immediately upon your arrival. This is by order of the fort commander, Tribune Lucius Caedicius. I'm to inform you the matter is extremely urgent."

Glaxus glanced around and spotted the headquarters building. He trotted over to the entrance, his ring mail armor suddenly feeling like much more than thirty-three pounds. It had been a long day and a long march. What could be so important? Once inside, he gave his name to the first guard he saw. The man went down the torch lit central hall and around a corner, returning a moment later to wave Glaxus forward.

Turning the corner, Glaxus stepped through a door and into the council room. It was larger than the one at Fort Vetera, with a higher ceiling. Varus and Tridonis were sitting uneasily beside each other at a long table. Also seated next to Varus was a tribune Glaxus hadn't seen before, presumably Lucius Caedicius. Several more tribunes stood against the walls, including those from the 19th Legion. Cornelius was directly behind Varus, glowering at Glaxus as usual. Plutarius stood under an oil lamp, his eyes expressing grave concern.

Something, somewhere had obviously gone wrong. This gathering wouldn't have been called if all were proceeding smoothly. Glaxus wondered nervously how he could be involved. As he'd done last time, he struck his chest and saluted the General. "Senior Centurion Glaxus reporting as ordered, sir."

Varus clearly wasn't pleased to see him again. "More than three months before I arrived in Germania, Centurion, a group of Gauls led by Segestes came to Fort Vetera to discuss the alliance. You were among those who met the chieftain and his delegation. You mentioned this at the last war council."

"Yes sir."

"Would you recognize any of those men if you saw them again?"

"I would, sir."

Varus gestured to Cornelius who took a basket from under his cloak. Knocking away the lid, the Tribune pulled out a man's head and swung it up to Glaxus' face.

"The Legate and the Chief Centurion remember him as one of Segestes' delegation. Do you? Speak up!"

Glaxus had to stiffen his body to keep from stepping back. "Yes, Tribune. He was one of them."

Cornelius thrust the head back into the basket. The General then pointed at the Legate without making eye contact.

Giving no acknowledgment to Varus, Tridonis addressed Glaxus. "A few hours ago, this head and its body were found buried in the woods near the fort as sanitation holes were being dug. Several other Gaulish warriors were found with it in the same condition, but this is the only one Plutarius and I recognized. They had not been in the ground long. As you can see, the head hasn't begun to rot. He's probably been dead less than twelve hours. We were not told his name when he accompanied Segestes that day, but we've questioned some Gauls in our auxiliary units and they tell us his name was Conrad. They say he was one of Segestes' most trusted counselors." Tridonis paused to lean forward in his chair. "So, Centurion, do you see the questions that confront us?"

"I believe so, sir. Why was this trusted advisor here and not down on the Erft with Segestes? Why was he killed and by whom?"

"Precisely. I asked the General to bring you to war council again so that you might confirm the memories of the Chief Centurion and myself, and also because you were concerned about the veracity of Herman's message. I felt you deserved to be here since that veracity is now in serious doubt."

"I think I understand, sir. You believe Segestes sent Conrad to tell us something."

"I do," said the Legate firmly.

"But you suspect Conrad and his group were intercepted and killed, possibly by Gauls working for Herman. If such is the case, sir, we can only assume Conrad was bringing a warning about Herman. I therefore respectfully restate my earlier recommendations. The campaign should be halted until we scout Herman's proposed route while at the same time we search for Segestes."

This set off a round of grumbling among the tribunes of the 19th. As Glaxus expected, the next voice he heard was Cornelius'.

"More unsolicited advice from the great bear-killer? Perhaps his attendance at war councils causes him to forget his status. As for Conrad's death, it was most likely the result of an internal dispute among the Gauls and of no concern to Rome. Possibly he was banished by Segestes for giving bad guidance. He could then have come here with a small group of followers hoping to sell his services to us. Before they were able to contact us, they may have been murdered by Gauls loyal to Segestes. The perpetrators might even be members of our auxiliary units."

In spite of his dislike for Cornelius, Glaxus had to admit this hypothesis was not implausible. Everyone present knew that feuds among Germanic tribes and individuals were common.

After listening to Cornelius, Varus turned to the Legate. "What is your response?"

Glaxus knew Tridonis had to answer as if he expected a fair judgment. "The Tribune's theory sounds as likely as mine, General. If you accept his guidance, we continue the campaign. If you accept mine, we wait, scout, and seek out Segestes."

Varus put on a show of looking thoughtful before making a decision that surprised no one. "We proceed as planned. As I said before, we have sufficient strength to meet anything the Gauls may attempt."

"But sir," said Plutarius, "we're unsure about the combined population of the tribes on this side of the Rhine. They could be living here in countless numbers. If Herman is planning a trap, we—"

"I'm coming with twenty thousand Roman troops. No ambush could possibly succeed. Besides, if Herman is not lying, we would offend him by disregarding his message, by rescouting his route, and especially by going behind his back to consult his father-in-law. The alliance could then be jeopardized along with the Emperor's ambitions for Germanic Gaul." The General stood up. "At dawn tomorrow we march north from here as Herman's route indicates. That's final."

Before Varus spoke again, Glaxus saw him exchange a brief look with Cornelius.

"Centurion, you told me recently that you're retiring after this campaign. How would you like to do so early and be on your way to Rome tomorrow?"

VI

These bastards Varus and Cornelius wanted to be rid of him! They must have begun scheming after the last war council and now Varus was using this opportunity to toss the bait. Glaxus was sure his letter to Calvinia had not been mentioned to the General by either Plutarius or Tridonis. Retirement and physical safety were the lures. The certainty of returning to Calvinia was an added inducement his enemies weren't aware of, but she wouldn't expect him to gain that assurance by trading his honor.

"No, General. I do not wish to retire early. I enlisted for twenty years and intend to fulfill that term of service to the very day. I expect the army to do the same." Then something occurred to Glaxus. "I would also have to insist that I not be left behind on garrison duty."

Varus frowned as Cornelius curled his lips in a silent snarl. Glaxus could see he had guessed rightly. If tempting him with early retirement failed, leaving him behind at Fort Aliso had been the alternate plan.

"I believe my nineteen years of dedication to the Emperor and his army have earned me the privilege of serving to my fullest capacity, right up until my commitment is completed."

"Not to mention his half-dozen commendations for valor!" The anger in Plutarius' voice was barely controlled.

"If I may speak, General." Tridonis stood up. "Your regard for the Centurion's welfare is most heartening, but I must agree that such concern is misplaced. Discharging or relegating to garrison duty one of our best at the start of the campaign would not only be an insult to him, but also demoralizing to the troops. Perhaps instead you will consider offering your concern to our friend

Cornelius. I'm sure those who remain at the fort on the garrison detail would welcome the Tribune's presence as much as we on the campaign would miss it."

Cornelius could do nothing but shift his glare from the Legate to Glaxus and back again. The General meanwhile found himself retreating before Tridonis once more.

"Of course the Centurion will accompany us on the campaign." Varus forced a smile in Glaxus' direction. "I merely thought that after long years of service he might wish to begin enjoying his retirement a bit early."

You're a lying son of bitch, thought Glaxus, but knew saying so out loud would get him executed. He wasn't going to do Varus and Cornelius that favor. "Thank you anyway, sir. Permission to withdraw?"

The General abruptly pointed at the door. "You may all withdraw. Council is dismissed."

Glaxus instantly turned and left. Why in Jupiter's name did Augustus put Varus in charge of this campaign? It would be hard enough with a competent commander, let alone a sniveling, backstabbing fool.

Leaving headquarters, he headed for the barracks area. There was still activity everywhere, though the sun was down now and the assembly ground had been lit with torches. He was passing one when he felt a hand on his shoulder. Expecting Plutarius, he turned to see Cornelius.

The Tribune's face was a grinning mask in the firelight. "So the great slayer of bears will not abandon us for the pleasures of Rome. How noble! Now the troops can rejoice, for victory is ensured!"

Glaxus noticed for the first time that although a little shorter, this man was just as stoutly built as himself. Cornelius was also some fifteen years younger. A formidable opponent, if it ever came to that. But there was one thing Glaxus had that he was reasonably sure Cornelius didn't.

"Speaking of victory, may I ask the Tribune how often he has stood with sword in hand and faced an enemy on the battlefield?"

Cornelius looked as though someone bounced a stone off his forehead. He recovered quickly. "Your experience may exceed mine, you plebeian dog, but I'm a patrician and the son of a senator!"

"None is an amount easily exceeded, Tribune. As for being the son of a patrician family, try explaining that to a Germanic warrior eager to cut your head off. Now if you will give me leave to depart your exalted presence, this poor dog must find a place where he can lay and scratch his fleas."

Glaxus shoved past Cornelius, forcing the Tribune to step back to keep his balance.

"Plebeian scum! Born above a shop! When this campaign is done I will shine so brightly in Augustus' eyes, he will have no choice but to name me his successor! Then you and your ilk will know their place and keep it!"

Though Glaxus was already close to insubordination, this was so outrageous he couldn't help but laugh. "Emperor Cornelius? Excuse me if I don't kneel just yet. After all, Tiberius may have something to do with the succession."

To this fact, Cornelius apparently had no reply. He merely grunted, "Lowborn trash!" and stalked back to headquarters.

Turning toward the barracks, Glaxus sighed deeply. He was too tired to concern himself any further with Cornelius. For now, he only hoped his cot wouldn't be too lumpy.

"Good evening, Centurion."

Glaxus had to squint for a moment to see Pindocles gliding along in the dark, his black robes making him nearly invisible between torches.

"So you arrived safely, Greek. Was there any work for you along the way?"

"Nothing challenging, I'm afraid. Only a few crushed toes for those foolish enough to walk too near the wagons."

"How disappointing. Perhaps next time someone will split their skull under a wheel and you can try stuffing their brains back in."

But the physician seemed in no mood for banter. "I was passing through the crowd on my way to the infirmary when I overheard your conversation with the Tribune. A most unreasonable person."

"That's for certain. He seems to hate without cause."

"Yes, I've encountered others with that propensity. They consider themselves the center of the world and all its doings, believing they were born for a special destiny. When reality intrudes on this belief, they find that unbearable and must lash out. Latin is too rigid to express it, but in my tongue the words are psycho and pathos."

Glaxus had learned a little Greek from Calvinia. "Psycho pathos," he repeated. "Mind disease?"

"Correct. In my experience it's far more difficult to cure than any illness of the body. Indeed, it's impossible. And there seems to be much about this campaign that reeks of twisted minds. Even Varus appears to share the Tribune's aversion to reality."

"What makes you think so?"

"Rumors are circulating among the auxiliary Gauls that certain bodies have been found. This would seem to indicate caution, yet the General gives no orders to postpone our northward turn. Have you any knowledge of these things, Centurion?"

Glaxus had to be careful. If it became known that he revealed without permission what was said in war council, it could give Cornelius the perfect weapon against him. "I can only say that we march north as scheduled. As for these rumors you mention, what you have heard is what you have heard." He knew the shrewd Greek would understand instantly.

Pindocles frowned and folded his arms. "Then may the gods of Olympus protect us."

Something inside the left cuff of Pindocles' robe flashed in the torchlight and caught Glaxus' notice. Sure of what it was, he pointed at the sleeve. "You depend on more than your gods for protection. May I have a look at it?"

Pindocles drew out the dagger and held it up. Its jewel encrusted handle was topped by a double-edged blade that had clearly been honed to maximum sharpness.

"Is it from Hispania?"

"Yes. I had it made when I was there several years ago."

That weapon combined with the physician's knowledge of anatomy could mean a very unpleasant experience for someone caught off-guard.

"Have you had that up your sleeve in all of your past encounters with me, Greek?"

As Glaxus expected, Pindocles' only response was a smile.

Glaxus had to grin himself. "I suggest you temporarily cover the handle and sheath in black wax. That will make it less noticeable against your robes."

Pindocles raised his dark eyebrows as he returned the dagger to its place. "Very clever, Centurion. You display a most Grecian cunning. I will follow your advice."

"And you might consider arming those among your assistants whom you thoroughly trust. Where we're going, it will be helpful to have someone with his back to yours, so to speak."

"I understand. I shall take that advice as well. Now if you will excuse me, the cold in this land is something I have still not become accustomed to. I bid you good-night."

"Good-night, Greek." Glaxus was also eager to get out of the cold. In his assigned barracks he found Tytho and several other centurions eating and playing dice. They had brought from the cookhouse one pot of chopped pork boiled with garlic and another full of wheat porridge. There were also loaves of round bread. After getting help to remove his ring mail, Glaxus was glad to eat and talk awhile before sleeping.

At dawn, messengers were sent to rouse all centurions with marching orders. When Glaxus reached his century's campsite, he was relieved to see the men awake and helping each other into their armor. Likas was walking among them, making occasional suggestions.

Glaxus called him over and told him things appeared to be satisfactory. "Well done, Optio. Did anyone require extra motivation?"

Likas glanced at the vinestick as he handed it to Glaxus. "A jab or two here and there, sir. Nothing to speak of."

"Very good. Have the men form up."

The civilians were to travel in the middle of the column with troops before and behind them. Glaxus' century was chosen to march at the very rear. "That part of the column is most vulnerable to attack," Plutarius explained to him. "I want my best century in that position so they can teach a lesson to any renegade Gauls who may want to get clever." Because of this, the sun was high when Glaxus ordered his men to fall in and begin marching. Tytho's century was immediately ahead of his.

During dinner the previous night, centurions stationed at Fort Aliso told Glaxus of leading patrols as far as twenty miles to the north. Beyond that, the route would be familiar only to some Gauls in the auxiliary units, but Varus would certainly be too arrogant to consult them. And since word of his scorn for their kind had doubtlessly filtered down, it was equally certain they wouldn't volunteer any information. However, Glaxus remembered again that before the General's arrival Gauls had mentioned marshes to the north. Why hadn't Herman indicated any such places on his map?

For the time being the terrain was firm and dry, although rather hilly. Herman's route seemed intent on keeping them out of the woods, forcing them to take a winding path. Glaxus had to concede this made sense. A column so large and with so many wagons could never struggle along among the trees.

Yet the forest wasn't far away. It towered darkly on both sides of the grass-covered trail. Patches of fog hovered in the branches while birds chittered and sang, their music lost in the column's noise. The air was filled with the creaking of wagons, the thumping of hooves, and especially with the babble of voices. Glaxus knew from experience this would change soon enough. People would get tired as the day wore on and talk much less.

Though someone had to do it, Glaxus would have been more comfortable had his century not been bringing up the rear. Yet from this vantage point the entire column could sometimes be observed, and when they reached a hilltop late on the first day, he didn't like what he saw. He called Tytho over and pointed down the valley that lay before them.

Varus was committing the same mistake he'd made on his march up from Rome. The column was being allowed to stretch out too far. The head of it couldn't be less than four miles distant, with troops and civilians trailing behind in a long, thin line. Glaxus told Tytho the column had to be made shorter and wider so as to be less vulnerable to attack. "But the General is complacent and undisciplined. He should also have cavalry soldiers riding up and down the length of the column to keep everyone apprised of where we are and what lies ahead. The stream we forded awhile back took us unawares."

"That it did." Tytho looked down at his wet sandals. "In fact, we've heard nothing from up front since we left this morning."

Glaxus could guess what was happening at the head of the column. Tridonis and Plutarius were most likely trying to reason with the General, but were hearing their recommendations countered every time by Cornelius and the other tribunes.

The sun was nearly touching the treetops before word finally came to dig entrenchments for the night's encampment. Tytho openly expressed disgust at the lateness of this order. Though also angered by its timing, Glaxus was further concerned by its being informally relayed down the column. Why was it not carried along by mounted messengers or signaled by the trumpeters? Passing an order from mouth to ear that many times could easily result in its being garbled. When sending troops into combat, is this how Varus would command and control?

They quickly decided that on this first night Glaxus' century would do the digging and set up the tents as Tytho's stood guard.

The need to hurry forced Glaxus to take some shortcuts, making the trenches shallower than he would have liked and the embankments lower. The tents had to be erected by torchlight. From the shouts and curses echoing in the dark, he guessed the entire column was in a similar predicament.

They were preparing the evening meal over campfires when a wagon came by to distribute kegs of water. Glaxus asked its Gaulish drivers what they knew of the terrain ahead. The two auxiliaries consulted each other in the Germanic tongue, then one spoke in Latin that was slow but clear.

"The ground is hard and dry until we reach the Teutoburg Hills, Centurion. We must turn east there to find Cherusci lands. There is a large marsh to the north of the hills."

"Then we'll have to pass between the hills and the marsh?"

"Yes sir."

This seemed to match Herman's map, except that the marsh had been omitted. An oversight? Perhaps, but Glaxus still wished Varus would see reason and send a cavalry unit ahead to do some scouting, especially in the hills. Another route might be found.

Tytho overheard the wagon driver and asked him a question. "What's the path like that leads between the hills and the marsh?"

"It is narrow and long, sir. At least ten miles."

Tytho turned to Glaxus. "Then going that route would stretch the column out even farther and thinner than it is now."

"Making us still more vulnerable, but that's the way we'll go because Varus is determined to follow Herman's map and nothing can change the General's mind." But even while saying this, Glaxus decided to try. "Where are you assigned?" he asked the driver.

"I am a slinger in the fifth auxiliary cohort of the 19th Legion, sir. Driving a water wagon is one of my non-combat duties."

"Your companion will take over for you on the wagon. You're going to the head of the column with one of my soldiers to give these facts about our route to Chief Centurion Plutarius."

The young Gaul exchanged a nervous glance with his friend before hopping down. "Yes sir."

Glaxus wrote a message on birchbark expressing his concern about the length of the column and the lack of scouting. He also asked Plutarius to listen to the Gaul, then use that information to alert Varus about the route between the marsh and the hills. To carry the message, he picked Sutonius, one of the five who fought bravely with Herman the day the century was ambushed. "Get some torches and take your auxiliary comrade to the Chief Centurion. Report back to me as soon as Plutarius so orders. Go."

Sutonius returned in three hours. "Sir, the Chief Centurion listened to the Gaulish auxiliary, then went into the General's tent with your message. He came out a few moments later to dismiss the Gaul and to give me this reply. He said I was to place it in no one's hands but yours."

Glaxus took the folded wooden tablet. "That doesn't explain why you were gone so long."

"Sir, the head of the column is a great distance from here. I would have run, but the ground is rough, and in the dark I couldn't—"

"I understand. Some food has been saved for you. Go get it."

"Yes sir."

Glaxus walked over to Tytho's campfire and sat across from him. "Did you hear?"

"Yes. The column must be thin as a string. Do you think Plutarius had any luck warning the General about that?"

"No one has so far, but let's find out." Glaxus untied the tablet and opened it. "By all the gods, it's not from Plutarius! It's from Varus and Cornelius!"

Tytho sat forward. "Are you sure?"

"It bears their seals and signatures." Glaxus held the message up to the firelight and began reading aloud. "Senior Centurion Glaxus, your concern for the safety of these legions is duly noted. However, sending soldiers to the headquarters tent with unrequested information crosses the line from concern to interference. I can question the Gaulish auxiliaries as well as you. In your message to the Chief Centurion, you speak of the column being too long. As

I told both him and the Legate, that is my responsibility. I will tolerate no further meddling from them or you. Look after your section of the column and leave the rest to me. Publius Quintilius Varus, Supreme Commander."

Tytho sighed and sat back again. "The vain old fool thinks he knows everything, and from what you've told me, those idiot tribunes are only making matters worse. What does Cornelius say?"

Glaxus read from the other side of the tablet. "Centurion Glaxus, why do you persist in your attempts to sabotage this campaign? Do you hope to prevent me from someday being Emperor? Turn down the position of Chief Centurion if it frightens you, but let those who can lead do so. Keep your place, plebeian, and stop intruding into matters that are beyond your ability and status. I will not warn you again. Cornelius Gaelius Tulvis, Senior Tribune, 19th Legion."

"Emperor someday? Hah! Another arrogant bastard! At least you tried, Glaxus. The truth is Augustus made a poor choice to command his Germanic legions, but it's too late now."

Glaxus stared vacantly into the fire. Should he have swallowed his pride when he had the chance and allowed Varus to retire him to Rome? No, because in addition to being cowardly and dishonorable, it would have been unfair to Tytho and the others he served with. He was relieved that the opportunity was gone.

"You're right, my friend. Too late now." Glaxus slipped the tablet under his armor. He decided he'd better keep it on his person for the duration of the campaign. It might prove useful in the future, if he had one.

Over the next few days, Glaxus figured that Tridonis and Plutarius must have finally talked some wisdom into Varus. The trumpeters began signaling the order to begin each evening's encampment. Also, cavalry troops brought word to the rear about what type of terrain lay ahead. To Glaxus' dismay however, the column got no shorter. The horsemen he spoke to told him it was still some four miles long, usually longer by the end of a day's march.

In the middle of the seventh morning word came they were nearing the Teutoburg Hills and would soon turn east. It had rained heavily at dawn while they were breaking camp and the ground was soft underfoot. This made for slow marching and slower wagons. Glaxus realized they would be a long time in that ten-mile corridor between the hills and the marsh. Being at the end of the column, it was after midday before he got a look at either.

The marsh was huge. How could leaving this off the map be an oversight on Herman's part? It stretched out of view to the left and was mostly treeless, with large patches of reeds growing up through the murky water. On the right, the heavily wooded hills rose up into the mist.

After Glaxus' century was about a mile into the corridor, a horseman rode up with orders to march more slowly.

"You're not serious!" said Glaxus. "Things aren't slow enough?"

"That's the order, sir. The civilians are having trouble maintaining the pace."

"What about the hills? Has anyone been sent into them to do some scouting?"

"No, Centurion. No such orders have been issued."

Tytho was marching beside his century a few paces ahead of Glaxus. He dropped back to express his outrage as the horse soldier rode off. "Varus takes no precautions at all! I have a mind to lead my men into the hills and do some looking around on my own."

"You heard the rider. No orders to do so have been given and Varus frowns on initiative. There's nothing to do but slow down." Glaxus pointed at the marsh. "Not like the Egyptian desert, eh?"

"Not hardly," said Tytho. "I wish we were back in Egypt right now."

After the pace of their troops had been reduced, Glaxus began watching the hillside, scanning for any flicker of movement among the trees. But the first motion outside the column to catch his eye was in the marsh.

It was a mallard, sitting quietly on the water.

At that moment the howling began, scattered at first, but soon echoing from the hills in waves. Seconds later, shouts in Latin erupted from the center of the column. Next came a noise Glaxus recognized as the impact of sword on shield, the sound of combat. He'd heard it too often to be mistaken.

VII

Tytho halted his century. "Glaxus! Listen!"

"I hear it. There must be tens of thousands. They're ambushing us at the center first. They expect our troops to converge there to protect the civilians. Then still more Gauls will charge down and trap us all between the hills and the marsh." Glaxus was sure that was Herman's plan. The century in front of Tytho's was already running forward. What other choice was there? The civilians couldn't be abandoned.

Drawing his sword, Glaxus pointed it at the hillside. "We'll take our centuries up and come around behind the Gauls. Perhaps we can attack and flee repeatedly, striking them hard, then disappearing into the woods. We may at least draw some of them away from our comrades."

"So be it," said Tytho. "Lead on."

"Everyone put down your pack poles," ordered Glaxus, "and remove your cloaks. Follow me in single file and stay quiet. Tytho, you bring up the rear."

The slope was steep, but the undergrowth light. About a third of the way from the hill's crest, Glaxus looked back and held up his hand. The two hundred stopped as one man. He waved his hand toward the ground and they crouched together. Tapping himself on the chest, he pointed ahead. Tytho saw this from the line's rear and nodded.

Picking his way around the trees, Glaxus crept toward the left. The roar of battle below was deafening and he could see the Romans were taking the worst of it. Unable to get organized into units, they were literally being pushed into the marsh by the enemy. Scores of Roman dead already floated in the bloody water, many of them women and children. The Gauls seemed to be rushing down the hillsides without end. Herman must have put together a huge league of tribes for the purpose of wiping out the legions, possibly as many as forty thousand warriors.

He suddenly saw Plutarius and Tridonis side by side in knee-deep water, swinging their swords for all they were worth. They must have been at the head of column, but had come to the center to help despite being past their prime for combat. He didn't see Varus or any of the Tribunes.

Proceeding a few yards further, he was surprised to discover about three hundred naked warriors kneeling behind an earthen rampart. Keeping himself hidden in a clump of ferns, he estimated they were no more than twenty yards downhill from him. Painted blue for war and wearing gold armbands, they appeared to be an elite group, probably all chieftains. They were likely holding themselves in reserve until Gaulish auxiliaries came to help the Roman civilians. They were sure to be especially savage to Germanic brethren they considered traitors. Glaxus wanted very much to see Herman among them, but couldn't waste time looking.

Returning to the two hundred, he made eye contact with Tytho and pointed downhill. Tytho nodded. Glaxus then waved the men forward. When they were in place behind the Gauls, he shook his javelin first, then his sword. The men understood instantly and shifted their javelins into throwing position. Glaxus glanced again at Tytho, who made a slashing gesture across his throat. Glaxus nodded in agreement. They would kill every chieftain here, taking no prisoners and sparing no wounded. The alliance had been willfully broken and Roman children were being butchered. For that, Gaulish leaders would pay.

He'd always trained his men to take careful aim and not throw wildly. Tytho had certainly done the same. Also, since the Gauls would be hit from behind, their shields would offer no protection. Glaxus held his own javelin ready and took a deep breath.

"Attack!"

The hail of iron-tipped shafts fell upon the Gauls with devastating fury. It appeared to Glaxus that nearly all two hundred struck a target. Impaled through their backs, the dying warriors fell instantly, spitting blood and clawing at their comrades.

"Swords!" yelled Glaxus, and led the charge down the slope.

Few of the chieftains had even drawn their weapons while lying in wait. Those not hit by javelins were seized by confusion at the sight of two Roman centuries coming out of nowhere. They tried to run but were quickly cut down. Glaxus disemboweled two and saw Tytho get three. The troops made short work of the rest, cutting throats, lopping off heads, and retrieving javelins. It was time to regroup and seek another target. Glaxus was about to issue this order when he heard Tytho shouting.

"It's turning into a massacre below!"

The area between the hills and the marsh had indeed become a killing ground. As Roman troops and Gaulish auxiliaries fell everywhere, the civilians became easy targets. An infant was impaled on a spear and held aloft as a trophy by a grinning warrior. Two others laughed as they sliced the fingers off a screaming girl to get at her rings. Glaxus had witnessed much horror over the years, but the spectacle below was beyond anything he could remember. And he realized he was only seeing part of it. The same carnage was going on for at least two miles in each direction.

Likas was by his side now. "Sir! The General is nearly captured!"

Following Likas to the far end of the rampart, Glaxus saw from there that the Romans had erected a circular barricade of oxcarts. It appeared to be manned by about four hundred troops. To his surprise, Tribunes from the 19th were commanding sections of the barricade and seemed to be acquitting themselves well. Cornelius was not among them.

Varus was in his chariot in the center of the barricade, sword in hand. Plutarius had managed to reach him and from this distance seemed to be pleading with him. Varus ignored the Chief Centurion, staring instead at the legions' three eagle standards that had been placed in his chariot. Glaxus was sure the General drew his weapon with suicide in mind rather than fighting, but why hadn't he done it? For a Roman commander to lose a battle and be captured alive was unthinkable.

Despite the best efforts of his protectors, the Gauls were on the verge of breaking through to Varus. Glaxus didn't like the idea of getting killed for the old fool, but saw no choice.

"Tytho, do you see?"

"I do. Our plan must change, I think."

"Yes. The standards must be saved and Varus talked into falling on his sword. Should the Gauls take him alive, they'll sacrifice him to their gods. If two tortoise formations start out, perhaps one will be able to break through to him. We'll also be drawing some Gauls onto ourselves and away from the civilians. That may allow at least a few of them enough time to escape."

"What of the standards?" Tytho asked. "Bury them?"

"If we can do so without being seen."

"Once the standards are safe and Varus is on his sword, what then? To the last man?"

"Most likely, but by Jupiter's balls, we'll take some of those bastards with us." Glaxus addressed the two centuries. "We are unseen here and might escape if we made a run for one of our forts on the Lippe. Yet can we live like rabbits while our comrades die like Romans? You heard what Centurion Tytho and I have proposed. The choice lies with each man. When the order is given, either join the tortoise or don't. Tytho and I will go down there alone if we must." He pointed to the left. "My century over here. Tortoise now."

The entire century responded, but more slowly than usual. Glaxus noticed resigned looks on many faces. Others appeared indifferent. Shields clanging together, the men formed the tortoise, and then waited in total silence for the order to advance.

Tytho watched Glaxus' century, then glared at his own. "Will you let them shame you? Tortoise now!"

Tytho's men also formed up with no exceptions, though one soldier hesitated before being yanked into place by a comrade.

"Bravely done, one and all," said Glaxus. "When we reach the General, we'll join those surrounding him. May Mars grant that we die well." It wasn't until he said the word die that he realized he was never going to see Calvinia again.

Never.

But he surely wasn't alone with such thoughts. "And may Vesta give safety and long life to those we leave behind at home. Now brace yourselves. They're going to hit us as soon as they see us, but we must advance at standard pace. Too fast and the formations won't hold. Tytho?"

Tytho entered his tortoise at its front. "Ready at your command."

Glaxus slipped into place beside Likas. "Forward."

The two centuries moved steadily down the hill and into the melee. Debris and bodies lay everywhere and the grass was slick with blood. With the footing treacherous and attack imminent, Glaxus began to doubt the General could be reached. Then he saw through an opening between shields that the enemy was not reacting as he expected. The sight of Romans in organized formations clearly took the Gauls by surprise. They must have believed most real resistance was over and little was left but butchery. They fell aside from the tortoises, staring wide-eyed as the two units marched with complete control toward the beleaguered General. Glaxus welcomed such luck, but knew it couldn't last.

As a cry of joy went up from the soldiers protecting Varus, a Gaul on a captured Roman horse rode into Glaxus' view. Despite his nakedness and blue paint, Glaxus immediately recognized him as Herman. He was holding the head of a chieftain whom the two centuries had killed on the hill. Pointing toward that spot, he shook the head and shouted something in Germanic.

It wasn't difficult for Glaxus to guess what Herman was telling his warriors. A few hundred of their best had been eliminated by a supposedly helpless foe. They had to renew their fury and direct it at the tortoises.

The effect of Herman's words was instantaneous. The nearest Gauls threw themselves at the two formations with utter abandon. Some pulled at shields as others tried to jam lances in between. When a pair of hands seized the top of Glaxus' shield, he chopped down with his sword, severing four of the Gaul's fingers. The man screamed and fell as the formation advanced straight over him. Glaxus stepped on his back and stabbed him in the neck.

The noise inside the tortoise was unbearable. Bellowing with rage, the Gauls were throwing everything they could find against the Roman shields. Rocks, tree branches, severed heads, even the bodies of children; all were hurled at the formations in a frenzied effort to stop them.

Glaxus yelled over his shoulder at his men. "Courage! Discipline! By all the gods, we're almost there!" At that moment half a dozen warriors suddenly wrenched Likas out of the tortoise. Glaxus dropped his sword and grabbed the collar of his optio's ring mail. Striving desperately to haul Likas back in, he lost his grip when a Gaul slashed his arm with a dagger. Likas managed to stab a warrior through the eye before being dragged off and killed. Another legionary quickly stepped into the gap beside Glaxus.

One more comrade dead because of Varus' stupidity, yet Glaxus knew there was nothing to do but keep marching. He briefly examined his wound. It was painful, but he'd taken worse. Seeing a Roman sword in the bloody grass, he snatched it up, then lowered his shield slightly to locate Tytho's formation. It was to the left and several paces ahead. A huge Gaul on a horse was riding back and forth beside it, howling and shaking a cudgel. The man seemed to be building his nerve to try something.

Risking further injury, Glaxus lowered his shield a little more and shouted over the din. "Tytho! Porcupine now!"

On his next pass, the Gaul leaped from the horse toward the interlocking shields that formed the tortoise's top. Intending to break it apart with his bulk, he was still in the air when Glaxus heard Tytho call the order for the porcupine. Javelin points protruded from the formation with dazzling speed. The leaping Gaul hardly had time to scream before being pierced through a dozen times. Shields parted and swiftly closed again as he was lowered into the tortoise. A moment later his body appeared on the ground behind the formation, which had never stopped advancing.

"Tytho's tortoise eats him up and shits him out!" But Glaxus was sure that if several Gauls leaped onto a tortoise all at once, the result would be very different. The sooner the barricade was reached, the better.

Tytho's century got there first. Breaking from formation, they clambered over the carts through a curtain of Gaulish arrows, losing five men.

Glaxus led his troops over next. "Keep your shields up! Not too fast!" But he still saw two claimed by arrows. His own shield was peppered with them, and another found its mark in his right calf behind the greave. After reaching down to snap off the shaft, he glanced around inside the barricade. The injured, dead, and dying were scattered on the ground. The smell of sweat mixed with blood was everywhere. Glaxus could barely hear his own words above the screams, groans, and clash of battle. He ordered his century to spread out inside the circle of carts and provide reinforcement where needed. Tytho's men were doing the same. Glaxus then headed for the center to find Varus.

The General hadn't budged from his chariot. He was still staring vacantly at the standards as Plutarius pleaded with him. Struggling to stay upright, the Chief Centurion held out one bloody hand while keeping the other over a severe chest wound. "Please, General! Give me your sword! The Legate has already fallen on his and you must do the same. You cannot be taken alive. I'll hold it for you. Please, sir! Time is . . . is . . ."

Glaxus managed to reach Plutarius and catch him just as he collapsed. "Chief Centurion!"

"Glaxus! I knew if anyone made it through from the rear, it would be you!"

"Tytho got his century through as well, but I'm afraid we can only delay the inevitable. Tridonis has killed himself?"

"Yes. I held his sword for him. He fell on it with no hesitation, yet I fear his example has gone unheeded."

Glaxus eased the Chief Centurion to the ground and confronted the General. "You once accused me of having an unroman attitude because I tried to stop Fabius from taking his life. He lost only one man. You have lost three legions and thousands of civilians. If you think yourself more Roman than I, the time has come to prove it. Accept reality and fall on your sword. The Chief Centurion is too weak now to hold it for you, but I will if you wish."

Apparently struggling to overcome his disbelief, the General finally managed to look down on the left side of the chariot. Someone was sitting there, muttering softly. Glaxus could only make out the words, "My Sylvia! Goodbye, my Sylvia!"

"Decimus," said Varus. "Stand up."

A muddy tribune staggered to his feet, nursing a deep wound in his right shoulder. Glaxus wouldn't have known his name, but recognized him as belonging to the 19th. He was another haughty young patrician and companion of Cornelius, one of those who resented Glaxus' presence in war councils.

Though what did that matter now? This man would also be leaving behind a sweetheart. "The General's moment has come, Tribune, and he would prefer your help to mine. Can you manage?"

Decimus appeared reluctant to look Glaxus in the face. "Yes."

The General stepped out of his chariot and walked to a clear patch of ground a few steps away. His dazed expression never changed as Decimus removed his breastplate and eased the sword from his grasp.

Dropping sorely to one knee, the Tribune held the weapon up with both hands. "Ready, sir."

The General took his helmet off and tossed it to the ground in front of Glaxus. Though Varus was inviting him to do so, he felt no temptation to put his foot on it. He picked it up and placed it in the chariot. "We'll bury it with the standards."

"And burn my body?" Varus asked softly.

"If there's time."

As Fabius had done, the General stared at the blade for at least a minute. He then spread his arms and fell onto it, impaling himself just below the sternum and knocking Decimus backward.

"At last!" moaned Plutarius. "Hurry, Glaxus! A pyre!"

"Yes sir." Glaxus helped Decimus off the ground. "On your feet, Tribune. Get some men together and gather any wood you can find, including the chariot. The General's body and that of the Legate must be cremated before they fall into enemy hands. Bury the helmet and standards beneath the pyre. The Gauls may not think to look for them there."

Decimus was flinching with pain, but still took offense at Glaxus' tone. "You see fit to order me about, Centurion?"

"We'll all be in the nether world shortly, young man. We can argue about rank there. Now will you do as I suggest?"

An expression of regret passed over Decimus' face. "I'll do it as well as I'm able."

"I know that." Then Glaxus thought of something else. "Can you tell me what has become of Tribune Cornelius?"

"Cornelius!" Decimus spit the name out. "When the ambush started, he and I were cut off from the column by a dozen Gauls. I was felled by a lance in the marsh, but instead of coming to my aid, Cornelius dropped his weapons and begged to surrender. He told the Gauls he could help them if they spared him."

"He turned traitor?" Somehow, this didn't surprise Glaxus.

"Yes. I heard him claim he could tell them how long the column was and how our troops were deployed down its length. I doubt if he could do them any real good, but they seemed to think a cowardly Roman was a fine joke and took him alive. I know nothing about him after that. I was left for dead, but managed to get up and rejoin the General."

Cornelius might have saved himself temporarily, but Glaxus was sure Herman would have him killed soon after the massacre, probably as a human sacrifice.

As Decimus went to find help with building the pyre, Glaxus knelt beside Plutarius and slipped one arm under his head. He'd been wounded by an arrow bursting through his ring mail and its point was still in his chest. Glaxus frankly hoped the Chief Centurion would die of this injury before the Gauls broke through the barricade.

"We're being slaughtered throughout the countryside? Tell me the truth, Glaxus."

"Yes sir. They're pursuing our people for miles around. They may need a few days to find and kill everyone, but time is on their side, not ours."

Plutarius coughed violently, spitting up blood and grimacing with pain. "All the warning signs were there and the General still let it happen. I showed him your message and implored him to question the auxiliary you sent, but to no avail. He and Cornelius wouldn't listen to reason. The blame is theirs."

"The ultimate blame must lie with the Emperor," said Glaxus. "A campaign to colonize this territory should never have been ordered, but once it was, Varus was the wrong choice to lead it. He was an arrogant, incompetent idiot who couldn't see past the end of his own nose, yet the Emperor picked him anyway. You and I are here right now because of Augustus."

"Treasonous talk, but true enough. Would you say it to the Emperor's face if you could?"

"Probably not."

"I wish to Jove someone would, but he's so all-powerful that no one has the courage to question his judgment. And that has been our undoing, my friend. We . . . We . . ."

Feeling the Chief Centurion's body go limp, Glaxus watched his eyes slowly shut. Unfortunately, there was no time to mourn. The only thing to do was try to get his body on the pyre with those of the Legate and General.

Glaxus stood and looked around for Decimus. The Tribune and a group of soldiers were using shovels to tamp down clumps of sod. At least the standards were buried. Hopefully, no Gaul saw it being done. Now the pyre had to be built above them. Glaxus released the horses from the chariot and began hacking at it with his sword. Haste was imperative. The soldiers defending the barricade couldn't hold much longer.

And they didn't. "Breach!" Tytho's shouting carried over the roar of combat. "We've been breached!"

Glaxus turned toward his comrade's voice. The Gauls had used tree trunks to batter aside several oxcarts and were surging through the gaps. The Romans tried to hold their positions, but the solid mass of warriors stampeded straight over them. Only Tytho stayed on his feet, a pocket of space forming around him as he made the nearest Gauls pay the price. A moment later, he was swept under as well.

Glaxus raised his shield and sword into position. The howling mass hurtled toward him, bristling with blades, spears, and clubs. He would join Tytho soon. The only question was how many of the enemy he could take with him.

On his left, he suddenly saw another Roman. "Sutonius! Are we the last?"

"Yes, Centurion, I think so."

"Then let us die fighting. Keep your shield up and stay low. Go for the belly."

"Yes sir."

As the Gauls came on, Glaxus saw one point a sword at Plutarius' body. No doubt the head of a Chief Centurion would be quite a trophy. He stepped in front of the corpse. They would have to earn it.

Glaxus slipped under the first spearhead and stabbed upward, splashing hot blood over himself. The Gaul wailed and went down like a log, causing two more to stumble and fall. Of these, Glaxus beheaded one while Sutonius split the skull of the other. The natural instinct would be to fall back under the onrush, but that's what the Gauls would expect.

"Forward, Sutonius! Straight down their throats!"

Side by side, they hacked their way through, the startled enemy yielding before them. Glaxus attacked the large warrior directly in front of him and the man responded by swinging a club at his head. Though able to catch the blow with his shield, he was still sent reeling back. As his opponent prepared to swing again, he remembered an old trick he'd been taught during his first year in the army.

He simply feinted for the belly.

The warrior's immediate reaction was to heave his shoulders forward, pulling his bare stomach back from the sword tip. Glaxus then whipped the blade upward and impaled him through the throat.

But the horde of Gauls soon trapped the two Romans against an overturned wagon. As he glimpsed Sutonius being pulled down, Glaxus suddenly had his shield ripped from his grasp. A fist knocked off his helmet. His dagger was snatched from its sheath and driven into his thigh. An axe caught him across the chest, tearing open both ring mail and flesh. Despite the pain, he felt no fear. With death a certainty, fear seemed meaningless.

When he tried to raise his sword again the weapon was kicked from his hand. Now unarmed, he wanted to let the next assault be the last, but a lifetime of training wouldn't allow that. As a Gaul lunged forward with a lance, Glaxus instinctively sidestepped the thrust and grabbed him by the beard, digging both thumbs into his eyes.

"Chew on this, you Gaulish scum!"

Dropping the lance, the warrior shrieked and struggled to break free. Glaxus then swiftly shifted his hands, grabbing his naked adversary by the neck and genitals. The man groaned and went limp.

Though bleeding badly, Glaxus felt defiance rise up in him and he began lifting. The other Gauls looked on in dismay as the helpless warrior was heaved aloft by the dying Roman. When Glaxus hurled their comrade to the ground at their feet, they fell silent. He then stood panting before them, his vision blurred with blood and his legs ready to fold beneath him. What were the dogs waiting for? Why didn't they end it?

Perhaps they needed some motivation.

Standing as erect as he could, he rammed his fists into the air and shouted with what little strength he had left. He shouted for Plutarius, Tridonis, Tytho, and all the others, even for Varus.

"Senatus Populusque Romanus!" His words rang out in the sudden stillness. "The Senate and People of Rome!"

Then they swarmed onto him, dozens of hands pressing him face down into the stinking, gory earth. He only hoped it would be swift. Spitting out a mouthful of blood and dirt, he heard himself whisper, "Calvinia."

A sharp blow between his shoulder blades knocked the breath out of him. As he gasped for air, a second blow fell on the back of his head and darkness swept over him.

VIII

He was in Rome with Calvinia. They were walking on the Campus Martius near the Tiber, watching it flow slowly past. She put her arms around him and said he must never leave her again. But even as she spoke, he heard another voice calling him away. Calling him back... back...

"Centurion Glaxus? Can you hear me?"

A tent. He was in a tent.

"Can you speak, Centurion?"

"Su—Sutonius?"

"Yes sir. This is the first time in two days you have opened your eyes. The Greek physician said—"

"Pindocles? He's alive?"

"Yes sir. He was hurt, but still able to tend you. After he stitched up your wounds, he gave you a potion to keep you asleep. He said rest was the only thing that could save you. He also sewed up my arm."

"Where is he now?"

"I don't know, sir. He said the Gauls spared him to look after their wounded. I think that's what they took him to do when he finished with us."

"But why were you and I not killed where we fell? Why were we brought here and our injuries tended?"

"We and a few dozen other Romans were taken alive and at first I didn't know why. You were unconscious, so I was told to carry you over my shoulders as the Gauls marched us to the other side of the hills. They have a stone temple there. Our comrades were—" Sutonius choked on his words, the memories obviously too much for him.

Glaxus had expected it, but it still horrified him. "Our comrades were sacrificed to the Gaulish gods?"

"Yes sir! Some were buried alive, others were burned at the stake. The Gauls tied some to an altar in the temple and disemboweled them. The rest were beheaded. You and I were being taken to the altar when their leader walked by and saw us. He said something in Germanic to our guards and we were then brought here. Sir, their leader is Arminius! A member of our century!"

"I know. He calls himself Herman now. Did he tell you why he spared us?"

"He said he remembered how he and I had been friends and had fought together that day our century was ambushed on patrol. Why he spared you, I don't know."

"This was the day before yesterday?"

"Yes sir. We've been kept here from then till now. We were brought our evening meal just before you awoke, if you're hungry."

"Very." Sitting up, Glaxus reached for the plate of boiled ox meat and began eating. The taste was even worse than the smell, but there was obviously no choice. Inspecting his surroundings, he saw that the tent was Roman, certainly part of the spoils taken by the Gauls. Through a tear in the side, he could see the setting sun. An oil lamp hung overhead and the ground was thickly covered with straw. Like Sutonius, he was wearing only his red woolen under tunic. It was badly ripped over his chest wound.

"What has become of our armor?"

"Pindocles removed it to treat our wounds, then some Gauls came in and took it."

Glaxus remembered the tablet containing the replies from Varus and Cornelius. "Sutonius, I employed you as a messenger one night during the march north. The tablet you brought me then was under my armor when the Gauls pulled me down in combat. Have you seen it?"

"I recall bringing it to you that night, sir, but I haven't seen it since. I was asleep when the physician got here. He had your armor off by the time I awoke. If he took the tablet, I didn't see him do so."

Perhaps Pindocles found it. Or it could have been lost and destroyed when Glaxus was pulled down. He ordered Sutonius not to mention it to anyone.

"I won't, sir."

"Now, tell me. Did you see Tribune Cornelius among those being sacrificed?"

"I don't know the tribunes by name, sir, but I don't think I saw anyone of that rank among them."

Could Cornelius have somehow survived and escaped? If so, he would have to face justice for his act of betrayal. But Glaxus realized how little that mattered at the moment. He and Sutonius might not survive much longer themselves. Perhaps Herman had their wounds treated so as to sacrifice them later.

"Is the tent guarded?"

"Yes, Centurion. Besides, we're in the middle of the Gauls' camp, surrounded by thousands of them."

"So it sounds." Glaxus could hear singing and shouting just a few yards away. A victory celebration, no doubt. Even if they escaped from the tent, they wouldn't get far. Besides, he was still weary and very feeble. He wasn't sure he could walk, let alone run or fight.

He lay back on the straw. They were at the mercy of their enemies. What was there to do but wait and sleep?

Glaxus was awakened by the tent flap being opened. The morning sunlight came streaming in and he looked up to see Herman and Thusnelda. They entered with two warriors, one of whom placed a stool on the straw. Herman sat on it while his wife stood beside him. She was wearing the bear amulet Glaxus had refused to accept. Her husband was still naked and covered in his blue war paint.

Sutonius had also been awakened. Herman pointed at him and said something in Germanic to the two warriors. They seized him and dragged him out of the tent.

"Centurion!"

"Courage, Sutonius!" Glaxus tried to stand, but his legs were slow to respond. "What are you going to do to him, you bastard!"

Herman fixed a steady gaze on Glaxus and responded in Latin. "I plan to release him with you. I merely had him taken to another tent so we can speak privately. Neither of you will be harmed."

"Release us?" Glaxus found this more surprising than calming.

"Yes. Your armor is being repaired for the trip. I've also ordered the badges and military decorations on it to be saved for you."

Thusnelda whispered in Herman's ear and they conversed softly for a moment in their own tongue. Herman turned to Glaxus and laughed. "My wife is concerned with your well-being. She has an attractive slave-girl who could stay here with you to nurse your wounds and provide you with certain other comforts. Will you accept this hospitality, Centurion?"

"No."

"I knew it. How could you when so many of your comrades lie dead? But my wife wouldn't listen." Herman spoke in Germanic to Thusnelda and she gave Glaxus a disgusted look. As she left the tent, her husband took the amulet from around her neck.

"She doesn't understand Romans," said Herman, "and neither do I. I'm still surprised at how easy it was to get Varus into the trap."

"Don't judge every Roman by Varus. He was a fool."

"Whom you all foolishly followed."

"Some of us had our doubts, but the Roman army functions on discipline. Under a good commander, there is nothing we cannot do."

"And under a bad one, you march to your doom like sheep." Herman waved his arm through the air. "We're still chasing down Roman stragglers in the surrounding countryside. The killing goes on."

"Women and children, too?"

"Of course. Just as Varus would surely have ordered his soldiers to do to us."

"I've never killed a child!" snapped Glaxus.

"I can believe that, coming from you. I'm afraid I'm not so noble. I personally took the lives of several Roman children. Their heads are on sticks in front of my tent. Would you like me to have one brought to you?"

"Rot in Hades, barbarian!"

Herman grinned. "Speaking of heads, we were able to prevent Varus' pyre from being ignited and I have his preserved in cedar oil. I'm going to send it as proof of my triumph to Marobodus, chieftain of the Marcommani. I want him to join me in a total attack on the Roman Empire, on the city itself."

Glaxus couldn't believe Herman was serious. "If you think you're just going to walk into Rome, you'd better reconsider. A cowardly victory up here is one thing, but conquering the city is another. Besides, this affiliation of tribes you put together won't hold for long."

"We will see." Herman got off the stool and squatted on the straw, putting his face close to Glaxus'. "As for being cowardly, that's an insult I will not bear. There are no rules in war. Who should know that better than a Roman soldier? I'm a patriot fighting for freedom. Your empire conquers nations and subjugates their peoples, forcing them to work your fields and die in the arena for your pleasure."

"And when your tribes aren't fighting Rome, they're making war on each other, the victors sacrificing or enslaving the losers. Some tribes even sell their fellow Gauls into Roman slavery." Glaxus reached out and weakly shoved Herman away. "Don't preach patriotism to me, you butchering hypocrite! That's a lie. All you care about is yourself and gaining power."

Herman sat on the stool again and shrugged. "So? Someone must wield power. Does it have to be Augustus? Why not a Gaulish world instead of a Roman one?"

"As you said, we will see."

"So we shall." Herman pointed at the stitches on Glaxus' leg. "Pindocles put you back together quite nicely. I did well to spare him."

"Where is he?" asked Glaxus. "You won't harm him?"

"He's tending to our wounded. He received a sword cut on his shoulder when we captured him, but that was because he pulled a dagger from his sleeve and sliced the ear off one of my warriors. He's full of tricks, that Greek. I'll return his weapon to him and release him eventually, though I'm certainly not going to tell him so just yet. In the meantime, we need his services. You and your comrades inflicted more damage on us than you know, even in defeat."

"Oh?" Glaxus spit into the straw. "What a pity."

"Yes, I'm sure you're most regretful. Though I must admit, the bravery and self-control shown by Tytho's men and yours was remarkable. I doubt there are two other centuries in the entire Roman army that could have crossed that battleground to reach the General. But I expected nothing less of my former brothers-in-arms. It was also your two centuries that surprised my chieftains up on the hill, wasn't it? Their bodies were still warm when I got there. I'll wager that was your idea. Am I right?" When Glaxus said nothing, Herman nodded. "Of course it was. That was a severe blow. Many clans are leaderless now. And then there was your individual courage when you had your back to the wagon. My warriors thought they were facing Mars himself. You would have been the special sacrifice on our altar had I not intervened."

"Why did you?"

"Because I never saw you behave unfairly. You gave me both gold armbands that day we were ambushed on patrol. You're also the finest soldier I've ever seen."

"Those are sentiments I cannot return."

"I wouldn't think you could. After all, I've wiped out three legions of your comrades. The 17th, 18th, and 19th are all gone. I also destroyed three cavalry regiments and six auxiliary cohorts of Germanic traitors. That's twenty thousand troops. The ten thousand civilian settlers were also eliminated. As I say, we're still pursuing a few here and there, but the bulk of the work is done. Thirty thousand Romans killed in three days. Impressive, wouldn't you say?"

"You praise yourself too highly, butcher. Hannibal and his army killed sixty thousand Romans at Cannae in only one day, and there were no civilians among them. It was also a pitched battle, not a surprise attack."

"So I've heard. But I'll take my small victory anyway, if you don't mind. Besides, over 225 years have passed since Cannae. The world needed to be reminded again that your empire is not invincible. And even after that triumph, Hannibal couldn't conquer Rome and was eventually beaten. Perhaps I am the new Hannibal and will succeed where he didn't."

"Don't count on it."

"And don't you count on my failure, Roman." Herman stood up. "By the way, we couldn't find the standards of the legions. My guess is they were buried somewhere to keep them out of our hands. You wouldn't know where, would you?"

Glaxus kept his face neutral. "No."

"I didn't think so." Herman observed him silently for a moment before throwing open the tent flap. "I have duties elsewhere. You and Sutonius will be released in a few days when you're stronger and after we finish off the stragglers. You'll be given food and should be able to reach one of your forts on the Lippe." He draped the bear amulet around Glaxus' neck. "Wear that on your journey and any Gauls you meet will know you're under my protection."

"Will you tell me something before you go?" asked Glaxus.

"If I can."

"Was Conrad a messenger sent from Segestes to warn us? And was it your men who beheaded him and his party? Also, do you know what has become of Tribune Cornelius?"

"Cornelius? I remember him. One of the least trustworthy men I've ever met."

Glaxus bit his tongue.

"As for what became of him, I can't say. If he was taken alive, he was either sacrificed or soon will be. Concerning Conrad, yes, my father-in-law sent him. I knew Segestes was loyal to Rome and that he suspected I was planning a trap. Just prior to the alliance and shortly before I joined your century, we had a conversation in which I mentioned to him that an ambush near the Teutoburg hills might be feasible. Segestes advised me against it and I pretended to agree, but I suspected he would eventually try to warn Varus anyway. I guessed he'd do so after I left on the scouting mission. Knowing Conrad was the trusted advisor who would be sent with the warning, I had a detail of warriors watch him with orders to follow and kill him if he left Segestes' camp and approached yours. My men couldn't take the heads with them, so they quickly buried them in shallow graves along with the bodies. Segestes feels Rome is needed here to provide stability and prevent intertribal warfare. I disagree and think we can manage our own affairs."

Glaxus had come to think the same thing, at least concerning this side of the Rhine.

"Farewell, Centurion Glaxus, and good journey to Rome. Tell everyone there what has happened in Germania, though the news will surely precede you. I suspect you'll find the city awash in despair and anguish. At least I certainly hope so!" Herman laughed once more. "Perhaps we'll meet on the day I march triumphant into the forum!"

Glaxus watched his enemy leave and wondered if Rome could truly fall to the Gauls again. They had sacked the city in the 363rd year after its founding, but that was almost four hundred years ago, long before Rome had achieved military might and become an empire. Could such a thing happen now? He remembered Quintar asking him what the world might be like without Rome.

But it was useless to trouble himself about that. He lay back on the straw, tired and sore. For the present, he could only let the gods worry about Rome's fate.

As Herman promised, he released Glaxus and Sutonius a week later. A group of warriors escorted them to the western end of the Teutoburg hills where they were given red Roman cloaks along with their armor. They were also supplied with food, weapons, and flint. A big Gaul then pointed over Glaxus' shoulder and grunted in crude Latin, "South. Lippe."

There was nothing to do but start walking. "Come, Sutonius. Let's go home."

Glaxus recognized the area. It was where the column had turned east to enter the corridor between the hills and the marsh. They'd seen decomposing Roman bodies everywhere since leaving the Gauls' camp and there were more here. Glaxus surmised this group tried to escape southward, but had soon been caught. Women, children, and men lay limply in the grass, some alone and others in heaps. Many were dismembered or headless. It was an unusually warm day and the smell was nearly overpowering. The only option was to keep moving and leave this horror behind.

Glaxus noticed Sutonius turning pale. "A little further and we'll be away from here. Can you make it?"

"Yes sir, I'll be all right. The bastards didn't show any mercy, did they?"

"None."

As they passed another tangled heap of corpses, a girl crawled out of it.

"By Juno's crown!" exclaimed Sutonius.

"Silence," Glaxus ordered. "Say nothing, do nothing." He judged the child to be about ten or eleven. Her leather dress was dirty and torn and her face badly scratched. She kept her blue eyes on him in a vacant stare, her filthy blonde hair floating in the breeze.

"Look at her features, Centurion! The little bitch is a Gaul!"

"I said be silent!" Glaxus took a few steps forward and crouched down. He didn't speak a word of Germanic, but he hoped that with his gestures and the tone of his voice he could convince her not to be afraid. "We won't harm you, girl." He held out his hands and she slowly came closer.

"You're Romans," she said in passable Latin. "My father told me to run and stay hidden until I saw Romans. I thought none would ever come."

"Then your father was a Germanic auxiliary," realized Glaxus. This would explain why she spoke Latin, as well as her need to hide.

"Yes. He and my mother were killed the first day. I hid in the forest at first, but soon warriors began searching through it, seeking those who escaped. So I started hiding under bodies. I didn't think they would expect anyone to do that."

"Very clever," Glaxus told her, though he wondered how she stood the smell. "You think like a soldier." And there was a soldier's calm about her that was disturbing in a child who'd gone through what she had. But then her parents had been dead over a week. Continuing to cry would neither bring them back nor keep her alive. "What have you done for food and water?" he asked.

"I would come out at night and drink from the little streams in the forest. I also found stale bread and dried fish in an overturned supply wagon, but there isn't much left."

"We have fresh food. You can share with us."

"Not with me!" snapped Sutonius. "I say we leave her here to starve! Or even better, nail her head to a tree!"

The girl gasped and stepped back. "But father said Romans would be my friends!"

"Your father was right." Glaxus stood and put his hand on her shoulder. "She'll come with us, Sutonius."

"But Centurion, she's a Gaul!"

"You heard her say her father was an auxiliary."

"Bah! A Gaul is a Gaul now! Death to them all!"

Glaxus was certain this attitude would soon be common throughout the empire. Yet as Plutarius had said, he could at least keep his own hands free of innocent blood. "More slaughter will accomplish nothing. She comes with us, alive and unharmed. Is that clear?"

Sutonius scowled at her again before reluctantly nodding. "Yes sir, though how will we explain her to any Gaulish warriors we meet? They may want to kill her on sight. Remember that Herman's clemency was extended only to you and me."

"A good point," admitted Glaxus. Warriors would still be eager to eliminate any Gaulish auxiliaries or their families. He was thinking about this when the girl spoke to him.

"Could we tell them I'm your daughter? That you thought me killed, but found me later?"

"With my dark hair and eyes? I don't think they'd believe it."

"We could say your wife was a Germanic Gaul and I took more after her than you." She slipped her hand into his. "Please?"

Glaxus considered it. Although Roman soldiers were officially required to stay single, informal marriages with Gaulish women were not uncommon. Roman commanders knew this, but would usually look the other way. Any Gauls they met would also know it. Passing her off as his child might succeed. If he managed to get her to Roman territory, he'd give her to a Gaulish auxiliary to be raised.

"All right, we'll say you're my daughter. Do you remember Fort Aliso on the Lippe River, where the column turned north?"

"Yes. Is that where we're going?"

"It is. Once there, we'll be able to find a family to take care of you. My name is Glaxus and his is Sutonius. What's yours?"

"Hilda."

"I've never heard that name before. What does it mean?"

"My mother told me it means child of battle."

Fitting enough, decided Glaxus. He glanced at his shadow. "There are still a few hours till midday. Let's cover as much ground as we can before then."

It got colder in the afternoon and stayed that way for the next several days. Upon Glaxus' order, Sutonius took turns with him letting Hilda wear their cloaks. She said little, occasionally asking

Glaxus about himself. He noticed her smile when he said he had no children. He also saw that she walked closer to him than to Sutonius. The young soldier spoke to the girl as seldom as possible, but showed her no further hostility.

Much to Glaxus' satisfaction, they encountered no one. At each sunset, they would stop and use the flint to make a fire. When the sky was completely dark, he would check their direction. The terrain seemed familiar, but he wanted to be sure they were headed south. "First you look in the sky," he told Hilda one night, "and find Ursa Major."

"The Great Bear?"

"Yes. He's shaped like a big ladle. After you find him, draw a line in your mind from the star marking the bottom front of the ladle to the one marking the top front. Extend the line for five times that distance in the same direction and you'll find the star of ultima Thule, the far north. It's the one star that never moves all night. As long as we keep it behind us—"

"We're traveling south?"

"Correct, and must eventually run into the Lippe and Roman territory. Another day's walking I would think."

Hilda put her hands around Glaxus' arm. "Yes, pater meus."

It was the first time he had ever been called "my father." He wasn't sure he liked the sound of it. He quickly freed his arm from her grasp. "You don't have to call me that as long as there's no one around we must deceive. Now get some sleep. We'll be starting at dawn again tomorrow."

The pained expression on the child's face made him wonder if he needed to be so abrupt. Had she not recently lost her real father? What would Calvinia think of him?

When Hilda put her hand in his the next morning as they began walking, Glaxus didn't pull away.

Sutonius stayed a few paces ahead all day, plainly anxious to see the river or possibly a Roman patrol. An hour before sundown they crested a hill and met one. The Junior Centurion leading it was stunned at the sight of them.

"More survivors of the massacre!"

"Yes," said Glaxus. "From the 19th Legion. We're not the only ones to make it back?"

"No sir. An optio and two legionaries have reached us at Fort Aliso. Perhaps forts to the west have found some as well."

"Take me to your fort commander, Tribune Lucius Caedicius. Tell him I'm Senior Centurion Glaxus Valtinius. He may remember me."

"Immediately, sir."

Glaxus was pleased to hear others had reached safety, but even before survivors brought the news, it must have swept over the countryside from one Germanic tribesman to another. When it reached those in the auxiliaries, it was surely passed along to the Roman commanders. It could even be known in Rome by now. Homing pigeons and dispatch riders would have been sent without delay. He was distressed to think that Calvinia might believe him dead, but there was nothing to be done except reach her as soon as he could.

It was nearly dark when they entered the fort. Glaxus asked the Junior Centurion to take Hilda to the cookhouse to get her some food.

She clung to Glaxus' cloak for a moment. "Will you come for me later?"

"Yes. We must find you a family to live with before I leave for Rome."

The girl said nothing, but Glaxus didn't like the look she cast at him. He hoped she wouldn't make parting difficult. She was a Germanic Gaul and belonged with a family of her own kind.

Glaxus and Sutonius waited for Lucius Caedicius in the war council room, the same one where Glaxus had seen Conrad's head. As the Tribune entered, Glaxus recognized him and recalled how he had sat silently beside Varus during that meeting.

When Segestes came in next, Glaxus wasn't surprised. The chieftain had certainly heard how Varus ignored the implications of Conrad's death, so he'd come to find out why. He stood grimly beside Lucius, his face revealing intense indignation at seeing his loyalty to Rome disregarded. His broad shoulders bulged under deerskin garments as he kept his hands behind him. Glaxus couldn't tell if he remembered their meeting at Fort Vetera.

Lucius spoke first, standing before the two survivors with folded arms. "So you made it back, Centurion. We have suffered a major disaster, true?"

"True, sir. General Varus and his officers are dead. The three legions under his command were wiped out along with all the civilians. It happened between—"

"—between a marsh and the Teutoburg hills. We know that from the others who escaped. They were near the head of the column and somehow managed to slip though the Gauls. Instead of choosing to die like Romans, they fled for their lives. Still, the cowards have provided us with a first-hand account. Perhaps you can give us some new details. Where were you in the column when you ran away?"

Glaxus gritted his teeth to keep himself from being insubordinate. Besides, a little boasting might be better than angry denials.

"Sutonius, your arm."

"Yes, Centurion!" Sutonius was obviously just as upset. He extended his right arm, displaying a line of stitches running from elbow to wrist.

"Now help me off with my armor and tunic."

"Yes sir."

When Glaxus stood bare from the waist up, Lucius calmly studied the fresh scar on his chest.

"Any others?"

"Yes, Tribune. On my legs and arm."

"And how did you come to be sewed up?"

"By Pindocles, the 19th's Greek physician, after we were captured."

Lucius picked up Glaxus' tunic and handed it to him. "My apologies to you both. I knew these things already, but I wanted to be sure of my information."

"You knew we'd been captured?" asked Glaxus. "How?"

Lucius pointed to Segestes, who took a birchbark scroll and a writing tablet from behind his back. "You're name is Glaxus. We met once briefly at Fort Vetera, yes?"

"Yes."

The chieftain held up the birchbark. "This letter was brought here yesterday. It was written in Greek to prevent anyone among my people from understanding it. Here is a translation into Latin, done by the Tribune's scribe." He gave the tablet to Glaxus. "Lucius was kind enough to let me see it. A most interesting message."

Glaxus began reading aloud. "To Centurion Glaxus of the 19th—I use my native language here because it is alien to the Gauls. I trust Tribune Lucius will have it rendered into Latin for you.

"Once again the Sisters of Fate have crossed our destinies. After first being shocked at seeing you still alive, imagine my further surprise when I removed your armor to treat your wounds and out fell a certain item. When I saw what it was, I realized its importance and concealed it beneath my robes where it is hidden still. I later saved the fevered son of a Germanic warrior and in return he agreed to smuggle this message out to Lucius at Fort Aliso. I heard of your release and reasoned that you would head there before traveling to Rome to retire. I am soon to be released as well and will likewise journey to the capital. Seek me there among my fellow Greeks. I will place the item in no one's hands but yours. You can then take it to where it must go.

"Also, know that he of the mind disease is alive. He was about to be sacrificed shortly after your release, but convinced some warriors he could be useful and they took him to Herman. He then provided information about the forts on the Lippe and the number of troops at each one. In exchange, he was given his freedom and travels to Rome at this moment. Herman has told him you survived and were released. Your death and the quick retrieval of the item are his immediate priorities. He has cursed himself constantly for writing it. He spoke to me openly of these things because he believed Herman would have me sacrificed, as did I. He thinks you have the item and intends to intercept you when you reach Rome. His family is rich and well-connected. Beware.

"I cannot bring the item to Fort Aliso. The Gauls will soon be mounting an attack in that direction. They plan to destroy all the forts along the Lippe. I will first travel overland to Aquileia. From there I shall sail south along the east coast of Italia to Ancona, then I'll go overland again to Rome. I suspect you'll take a more westerly route.

"It would be safest if we arrived before your enemy, but that would not seem possible. He will surely be in Rome ahead of us both, and you will likely be there before me. This will prolong your danger, but you must stand fast. I shall proceed with all haste. May the gods of Olympus guide our efforts.—Pindocles."

"Obviously," said Lucius, "we're curious to know the identity of this person with the mind disease. And what is the item he wrote?"

"He's Tribune Cornelius and the item is a tablet containing replies to a message I sent to Varus. The General's response along with that of Cornelius would be of keen interest to the Emperor. They—"

"Stop," Lucius ordered. "Wait while I have the scribe fetched. I want you and the legionary to recount all you saw, heard, and did from the time the legions left Fort Vetera. You must omit nothing and add nothing, nor must you be modest. The scribe will set it all down in tablets which I will send to Rome with you, Centurion, along with this letter from Pindocles. Legionary Sutonius will be reassigned to this fort."

"And I will take my leave," said Segestes. "Perhaps I might yet prevent my countrymen from pushing south."

"I wouldn't think so," Glaxus told him. "Herman has them flush with victory. He's even talking of invading Rome itself."

"Prepare to evacuate with us, Segestes." Lucius' tone was blunt. "Going out to dissuade them would be courageous, but futile. They're in no mood to listen."

The deep sadness Segestes showed upon hearing this made Glaxus feel sorry for him. The chieftain must have genuinely hoped Rome would bring peace to his people, but all it had done was give them a new enemy to fight. Even if Rome repelled the threat of invasion, it would probably never again try to occupy territory east of the Rhine. Segestes had to know the tribes would then return to warring among themselves. He gazed at Glaxus for a moment, then at Lucius. "I will prepare for evacuation," he said softly, and left the room.

Glaxus and Sutonius sat with Lucius and the scribe for several hours, the Tribune constantly asking for particulars and thorough explanations. Glaxus had never seen a young officer so dedicated and serious, so interested in finding the truth rather than building a career.

Glaxus told all he knew, including the message he'd sent by way of Sutonius and the replies it provoked. He also related what Decimus told him about Cornelius' cowardice and betrayal. Lucius found this interesting because it confirmed what Pindocles had written. The Tribune seemed especially fascinated by Glaxus' conversation with Herman. "Details, Centurion," he kept repeating, "details." Glaxus then listened to Sutonius describe their last stand against the overturned wagon, their capture and narrow escape from sacrifice, and finally the discovery of Hilda during the return to Aliso.

Fourteen wax tablets had been filled by the time Lucius was satisfied. After dismissing Sutonius and the scribe, he spoke privately to Glaxus. "Tomorrow you will be on your way to Rome, Centurion, and these tablets will go with you bearing my family seal. I will also include a complete description of the war council that was held here. I vividly remember the arrogance of the General and Cornelius as they disdained your advice. Augustus will read that and the doctor's letter with great interest."

"Do you think word of the massacre has reached the Emperor by now?" asked Glaxus.

"Undoubtedly. I released the pigeons myself. And now that he knows, he'll want all the information about it he can get, though learning that his trust in Herman was misplaced will be painful for him."

"I will take the tablets to the Prefect of the Praetorian Guard?"

"Yes. His name is Seius Strabo. He will give them to the Emperor. You must do the same with the incriminating tablet as soon as the doctor gives it to you. I would send an escort of soldiers with you, but I can spare no one now. So you must be wary in Rome. The doctor is right about Cornelius' family being powerful. And since this information would cause them great shame and embarrassment in the eyes of Augustus, they will likely join Cornelius in trying to prevent such exposure. But the tablet Pindocles carries is most crucial. Without it, the situation would only be your word against Cornelius'. That would not be enough for the Emperor."

Glaxus hadn't thought of this. "The word of a lowborn plebeian wouldn't stand against that of a patrician?"

"Exactly. And if Cornelius were put on trial for treason before the senate, I'm sorry to say your testimony wouldn't carry much weight there either. The physician must get that tablet to you so you can get it to the Prefect. The truth must prevail. Myself and other Roman soldiers may face death because of Cornelius' treachery."

Glaxus felt the impact of Lucius' words like a blow. "I swear to you, sir, if Pindocles reaches me with the tablet, only my own death will keep it from the Prefect."

"I don't doubt that for a moment. What I want to know is why Pindocles is willing to step into this cauldron. He could have simply destroyed the tablet."

"He's a proud man and wasn't pleased when Varus demoted him in favor of some Egyptian physicians. Revealing the General's stupidity would be just the sort of revenge the Greek would enjoy."

"He'd best be careful. If he let's word slip out during his journey that he has something damaging to a great Roman family, his life may be in danger. There are those who would kill for it that they might use it as an instrument of extortion."

"Pindocles keeps his mouth shut better than anyone I've known, Tribune."

Lucius shrugged. "As you say, but many a tight tongue has been loosened by wine, women, or gold, and there's no shortage of those on his route to Rome. You also must be silent about the tablets you carry, lest you become a target for the same reason. The scribe will make copies which I'll keep, but it's vital for that information to reach the Emperor."

"Yes sir, but your jeopardy here is equal to any I may face. Herman will almost certainly attack this fort first. What will you do?"

"We're preparing to make a defense, but if our scouts report the enemy force is too large, we'll evacuate to Fort Vetera. Tribune Monius Asprenas is coming north with two legions from the junction of the Rhine and Main rivers. Even if we lose the Lippe forts, Asprenas will hopefully be able to keep the Gauls from crossing the Rhine. I also suspect the Emperor will recall Tiberius from the Pannonian revolt and order him to return here."

Glaxus had never seen Tiberius, but every Roman knew he was likely to be Augustus' chosen successor. He was the Emperor's son-in-law as well as legally adopted stepson. Possibly the finest commander in the army, he would certainly have his hands full if he returned to Germania.

"And now, Centurion, you must eat and rest. You have a long journey before you." Lucius grinned broadly at Glaxus. "And may the gods grant that Rome is no less peaceful for you than was Germanic Gaul!"

IX

Glaxus discovered Hilda still in the cookhouse, wide-awake despite the late hour. She was surrounded by several members of the century that had found them. Wearing the Junior Centurion's helmet and listening carefully to his instructions, she advanced across the floor with a wooden training sword.

"Like this, Vadorius?"

"No. Thrust, don't slash. And right foot forward."

Though most of the soldiers smiled as they watched, Glaxus noticed a group of half a dozen standing by the rear door. They glared darkly at the girl, saying nothing. This was no surprise. She was a member of the race that wiped out their comrades. They looked at her as Sutonius had, as many Romans would.

But to the others in the room, she seemed to be only an innocent child whose enthusiasm at being in their company had won them over. Glaxus sat at a table and took off his helmet and cloak. "Would you make an Amazon of her, young man?"

Vadorius laughed. "No sir, but perhaps a gladiator. I once saw two women fight in the arena at Narbo. It was most entertaining."

"No doubt." Glaxus could still smell cooking in the room. "Has she eaten?"

"She has, sir. Would you like something?"

"Indeed."

"Food and drink!" said Vadorius, and a soldier quickly brought Glaxus a steaming bowl of gruel with a cup of hot wine. Vadorius then slipped his helmet off Hilda. "It's time my men and I retired, sir. A cot has been prepared for you in barracks nine."

"Very well, but stay behind a moment."

"Yes sir."

Hilda waited until the soldiers filed out, then sat close to Glaxus. "Where will I sleep?"

"That's what I want to speak to your new friend about." Glaxus looked him over and knew he hadn't been a centurion for long. "When were you promoted from optio?"

Vadorius suddenly seemed self-conscious. "Only a month ago."

"A heady feeling, eh?"

"Yes sir. It certainly is."

"It wears off soon enough, I can assure you." Glaxus glanced toward Hilda. "Do you know a place where she can sleep safely tonight?"

"The fort's physician and his wife have a daughter about the same age. I don't believe they'd object to a one-night visitor."

"I also need to find her a Germanic family to live with."

"There's a cohort of Germanic auxiliaries assigned here, sir. I'm sure you can find a family to take her. Now, if there's nothing more, I must check on my men in their barracks. Good night."

"Good night, and thank you."

"When are you leaving?" Hilda asked after Vadorius was gone.

"Tomorrow morning," said Glaxus.

"Will you say farewell before you go?"

"Of course."

She stood up. "Would you take me to the physician's now? I'm tired."

He'd hoped she wouldn't cry to go with him, and she hadn't. She'd stay with her own kind, he'd return to Rome, and that's how it should be. Yet as he peered into her eyes, he began to have doubts.

"Is staying here with a Germanic family what you'd like?"

"No. I'd rather go with you, but I haven't said so because I know you'll refuse."

Glaxus asked himself what Calvinia would want. She had no children and was past the age for bearing them. That Hilda was not from Italia would mean nothing to her. She'd surely want him to bring the girl.

But what of his own wishes? Was he willing to accept this responsibility? Even if he were, Cornelius might be waiting in Rome to kill him. Could Hilda withstand losing another father? Yet suppose he left her and Herman's horde stormed the fort. Would she have survived the massacre only to die here?

Glaxus stood up and held out his hand. "You will come with me. In Rome there is a woman named Calvinia whom I intend to marry. We will adopt you."

Hilda took his hand in both of hers. "Yes, pater meus."

"But when we first arrive, we could find danger there as well as here. You may have to be brave again, as you were in the forest."

"I'll do my best."

He nodded. "Then we leave in the morning."

At dawn, Glaxus reported to Lucius in the headquarters building. He was given a leather pouch containing the tablets he and Sutonius had dictated, along with Pindocles' letter and Lucius' description of the war council. Lucius also gave him some traveling money.

"You'll be going to Rome with a large group of civilians, Centurion. When my troops and I are withdrawing from the fort, I don't want to have to worry about non-combatants, so I'm evacuating them now."

"Then there has been some sign of the Gauls?"

"Yes. Cavalry scouts returned late last night after I spoke with you. Germanic tribes are massing halfway between here and the Teutoburg hills. Apparently they've finished mopping up stragglers from the massacre and are getting ready to push south and west, so I gave orders to get the civilians out today. I'll march my troops to Fort Vetera tonight."

Glaxus again admired Lucius' professionalism and became concerned for his fate. Of senatorial rank by birth, he risked much by informing the Emperor so bluntly of Varus' vanity and incompetence. The General had been a close friend of Augustus and a member of the imperial family through marriage to the Emperor's niece.

Even if Lucius survived the Gauls' attack, he might still be in danger, for how would the Emperor respond to such harsh honesty?

"Good luck getting to Vetera, sir, though I think you'll most need fortune on your side if you make it back to Rome." Glaxus patted the pouch.

Lucius understood, but only smiled. "I've met Emperor Augustus. He can rule with an iron hand when he must, but he's not a vicious tyrant, and he's not afraid of reality. The preservation and stability of the empire are more important to him than anything or anyone, including members of his family. Besides, all Rome knows by now what a fool Varus was. That pouch contains more of a risk to Cornelius than it does to me. Your account of the Tribune's behavior during the campaign would cause him and his entire clan to fall out of favor with Augustus. And if the Greek arrives with the final tablet, their disgrace would be unendurable. It is you and Pindocles who will need luck in Rome, Centurion. Now be on your way and safe journey to you."

Glaxus went to the infirmary to get Hilda. Having been scrubbed and given warm clothes, she grinned happily as she was brought out to meet him by the physician's wife. They then found seats on one of several wagons outside the main gate. He spoke with some of their fellow travelers and learned the route would not be overland all the way to Rome. The roads had to be kept clear to allow troops to march north. They would instead cross the Alps to Cemenelum, capitol city of the Maritimae province, then sail south down the west coast of Italia to Ostia. From there it was a short barge trip upriver to Rome.

Glaxus estimated the entire trip would take between thirty-five and forty days, depending on the weather. The sea voyage alone might be up to ten days. He didn't look forward to that part, though it occurred to him that traveling by way of Ostia would give him an opportunity to see Macro. Perhaps his friend might go with him to deliver the pouch.

The trip over the Alps was slow and cold. The frigid air made Glaxus' wounds ache. Though most of the inns they stayed at were hardly more than shacks, he was glad to reach one every night and sit before a fire. Hilda stood out sharply from the Roman children in the group, drawing occasional stares but no remarks. Glaxus never let her out of his view, always going with her to their small, dirty rooms and waiting until she was asleep before lying down himself. One night she began crying in her dreams and calling for her parents. He sat on his cot and listened, wondering what to do and feeling helpless.

He had been a soldier his whole life and knew nothing of children. He gently brushed a strand of hair from Hilda's face and realized he'd need Calvinia more than ever. "But she must think I'm dead," he whispered. "And if her shop is failing, she may change her mind and marry Hyboreas out of desperation." He sighed and shook his head, knowing there was no option except to hope against such a thing and keep moving toward Rome.

Upon their arrival in Cemenelum, Glaxus immediately began looking for sea passage to Ostia. The waterfront was crowded, smelly, and loud, though to Hilda it was a fascinating spectacle. She trotted alongside him on the docks, watching intently as ships loaded cargo and boarded passengers.

"Are all these people going to Rome?" she asked.

"Most of them. They hope they'll be safer there if the Gauls sweep down from the north. But some are going to cities all over the empire. We must find a ship bound for Ostia. That's the port town that serves Rome."

The multitude of travelers parted smoothly before Glaxus as he strode along in full battle dress, his red cloak billowing in the ocean breeze. There were hand-painted signs before each ship declaring where it was going and when. Seeing a corbita that would soon be leaving for Ostia, he got in line behind the other people waiting to embark on it. As they noticed him, they stepped aside, allowing him to lead Hilda up the boarding plank. "Hail, Centurion!" said several as they waved him forward.

He took such attention lightly. All military men would be popular now that the empire faced a major crisis. Forgotten in peace and appreciated only when called on to fight and die; he was sure that would forever be a soldier's lot.

When Glaxus asked if there was room for two more, the captain opened his manifest tablet and nodded vigorously. He was a wiry little man with no hair at all and a voice like a crow. Hilda gazed at him in amazement.

"Yes, yes, room for all. We take only passengers on this trip and no cargo. Everyone will be packed together like mackerel in a barrel, but it's friendlier that way, isn't it? Five aurei for you, soldier, and four for the little one." He jabbed his hand out. "In advance, if you please."

Glaxus considered this a bit steep, but with so many people wanting to reach Rome, he knew captains could name their price. He handed over the coins and wrote their names in the ship's manifest.

They were underway with the tide that afternoon. In spite of calm seas and a fair sky, the captain kept the ship in sight of shore. It was November now and storms could arise from nowhere. Glaxus knew this, but hoped they would be lucky and have smooth sailing the entire way. His stomach was already somewhat queasy.

To Hilda, however, it was a grand adventure. Never having beheld the sea before, she asked him dozens of questions about how big the Mediterranean was and what points on shore they were passing. When he couldn't tell her, she asked the captain and crew. She wanted to understand how the great square sail was raised and lowered and the way the ship was steered. At night she looked at the stars as Glaxus had taught her and told him in which direction they were going. One morning when the wind was brisk and the ship making good speed, he took her forward to watch the dolphins leaping along before the bow.

"Oh, pater meus! It's all so wonderful!"

"Yes, it is." Though he doubted he'd have thought so were she not with him.

Still, the realities of sea travel had to be confronted. The vessel's tightly cramped sleeping quarters came as no surprise to Glaxus.

Its sanitary facilities were also as miserable as he expected. Yet Hilda's enthusiasm never wavered, and by the fourth day her interest had shifted to the city of Rome.

"How many people live there?"

"About a million."

"Do they live in large, beautiful houses?"

"Only a few do. Most live in insulae, huge buildings full of rooms with a family in each one. They're crowded, noisy, and dirty."

"Will we live in such a place?"

"We may have to for a short time." Glaxus was reluctant to do this. The typical insula was a poorly built wreck ready to collapse under its own weight or burst into flames. Being entitled to some land as part of his retirement pension, he planned to move onto a small farm north of the city. How long this would take to arrange he didn't know.

"And where do a million Romans get their water?" Hilda wondered next.

"It flows down from streams in the hills through aqueducts. People fill jars at fountains in the streets."

"It's brought that close?"

"Yes. Just a few steps away no matter where in the city you live. In the great mansions water is carried all the way inside through pipes."

This was too much for Hilda and she stared at Glaxus in awe. He put his hand on her shoulder. "Be patient, filia meus. You will shortly see Rome for yourself, both the good and the bad." He hadn't called her "my daughter" before now. He was surprised at how naturally the words came.

The corbita dropped anchor off Ostia on the ninth morning and ferries rowed out to collect the passengers. Not far away, grain ships from Egypt were being unloaded by slaves carrying basketfuls onto barges. When Glaxus set foot on the docks with Hilda, he realized the time for vigilance had come. He shouldered the woolen bag holding their few belongings while pressing his elbow against the leather pouch under his cloak. Grasping Hilda firmly by the hand, he leaned down to her ear.

"Stay close to me always. There may be people about who won't be pleased to see us because I bring news that will cause them harm. Do you understand?"

He felt her hand tighten on his. "Yes, father."

"But before we go up to Rome, we must find a friend of mine. He should be in Ostia by now."

Glaxus asked a group of dockworkers about Macro and was told he and his uncle ran their business from a warehouse on wharf seven. Glaxus found him there, arguing with a barge captain about how many jugs of wine should have been unloaded.

"You were supposed to pick up thirty from that last ship! You'd better not be stealing from me, you son of a whore! Count them again!"

"Count them yourself, Optio."

Macro turned and saw him. "Glaxus! By all the gods, you're alive! I feared you dead in the massacre!"

Glaxus seized his friend's forearms. "I sometimes can't believe it myself, Macro. I have more to tell you than you can imagine."

"And I, you. I have seen Calvinia. Come into the warehouse and we'll talk. You're slave girl can wait here."

Glaxus put his arm around Hilda and drew her close. "She's not a slave. She's soon to be my legal daughter."

Macro scrutinized her closely. "But she has the look of a Germanic Gaul."

"She is. Her name is Hilda. As I said, I have much to tell you."

In the warehouse, Macro chased away his workers and swiftly cleared stacks of tablets from a table. He then poured two cups of wine and set out bread and fruit. As he and Glaxus sat down to talk, Hilda perched nearby on a sack of corn, eating a fig while she listened.

"Tell me of Calvinia. Did you give her the extra copy of my letter?"

"Yes, and a good thing, too. The first hadn't yet reached her. She went to the room above her butcher shop to read it, and came down again a few minutes later. Whatever you wrote seemed to agree with her. She asked anxiously about how dangerous the campaign would be and when you might return to Rome."

"This visit was before news of the massacre?"

"Yes. She must be in despair now, thinking you were killed. You need to reach her with all haste."

"I intend to. Tell me, Macro, does her shop do well?"

"The only customer who came while I was there was a crippled old man. He wanted a pig's leg, but had only half the price. Calvinia let him have it for that and told him to pay the rest when he could." Macro grunted in disapproval. "I think she was too long a patrician. Such generosity would put me out of business in a day."

Glaxus smiled, knowing Calvinia couldn't do otherwise. "Is she receiving the bread dole?"

"I asked her. She's not eligible because she's an unmarried woman with no children. She'd probably be too proud anyway."

"True enough," admitted Glaxus. "Now, are there any barges headed to Rome today?"

"I have one going up this afternoon, and when you arrive, you'll hear everyone still talking of the massacre. The Emperor has disbanded his Germanic bodyguards and now relies solely on the Praetorians. He's also insisting that all able-bodied men register for army service, but the response is weak. No one can believe what's happened, so no one thinks they need to serve. They find it hard to accept that an emergency is upon us. It's been so long since there was a direct threat to the capitol that it seems inconceivable. And veterans are being recalled, as well. You may not be allowed to retire, Glaxus."

The possibility of being sent back to Germania hadn't occurred to Glaxus. He would have to see Calvinia before going to the Prefect. If he didn't see her now, perhaps he never would.

"And I thought there would only be a skirmish or two east of the Rhine," said Macro. "I was a fool. Tell me how it happened."

Glaxus told the entire story, including the finding of Hilda and finishing with the pouch and its contents. "Will you join me in taking it to the Prefect, Macro? An extra pair of eyes to keep watch would be welcome."

"Of course I'll go with you, though I can offer you only one extra eye."

This remark startled Glaxus into remembrance. "Of course! The bear! But I see an eye where none should be."

"It's glass. I had it made in Rome because I got tired of wearing a patch. Quite fashionable, eh? And having a handicap keeps me from being recalled in this military emergency."

Hilda slipped off the corn sack and stood in front of Macro. "It looks real."

"See for yourself, then." He squeezed out the glass eye with his left hand and placed it on her palm.

She peered studiously into his empty socket, then slowly rolled the eye between her fingers before returning it to him. "I'll call you Uncle Cyclops."

"Fair enough!" declared Macro, and rubbed her head. "Listen, Hilda. There's something I must speak to Glaxus about. While I do that, you can go find Ajax. He's the worthless old cat we keep in the warehouse to amuse the mice. There's nothing he likes more than having his fat belly scratched."

She hesitated. "What's a cat?"

Glaxus held his hand low over the floor. "A little animal about this size. He won't hurt you."

As Hilda tiptoed between a row of barrels, Macro replaced his eye and lowered his voice. "If Cornelius has trouble waiting for us in Rome, taking the child along may not be wise."

"I was thinking the same. Do you know a place where she can safely stay until things are settled?"

"With my uncle and his wife here in Ostia. They already have five children of their own and won't mind one more. We must also decide what to do for her should the worst befall us. If you're killed, I'll raise her. If we both die, my uncle will. I'll arrange that before we leave."

"Thank you, Macro. I wouldn't want her abandoned on the streets."

"It won't happen, I promise you. Let's be on our way."

After turning over control of the warehouse to his foreman, Macro led Glaxus and Hilda to the insula where he lived with his uncle's family. To Glaxus' surprise, they occupied every room on the first level.

"You can afford to rent an entire floor?"

"Our business prospers," Macro explained. "And with all the children, we need the space."

While Macro spoke with his uncle, Glaxus took Hilda into the building's central courtyard and explained that she would have to stay here for a day or two. He thought it best to be completely honest with her. "As you know, certain people in Rome will not be glad to see me."

"I've heard you speak of someone called Cornelius."

"Yes. Because of him, danger may await me in the city, so I cannot bring you along now. If all goes well and I survive, you'll visit Rome with Calvinia and I. Then we'll go to live on a farm a few miles to the north. If I do not survive, you'll live here. Whatever happens, you must be strong."

"I will, pater meus, but please be careful." She put her hands on his shoulders as he knelt before her. "I could be stronger with you than without."

After taking Hilda to meet Macro's nephews and nieces, Glaxus waited in the courtyard. Macro came out wearing a toga with another draped across his arm.

"Glaxus, I suggest you wear this over your armor. I've done the same. There's a hole in it so you'll be able to reach your sword quickly. Your helmet and cloak can go in your woolen bag. This way no one will know you're a soldier. You can take it off when you report to the Prefect."

Glaxus thought this a wise precaution and quickly complied. Within an hour they were on their way up the Tiber. The barge was owned by Macro and his uncle and carried marble from Numidia. The slaves towing it strained against the river's current, grunting out clouds of breath in the damp air. Glaxus counted only ten of them on the ropes.

"That doesn't seem quite enough for so heavy a load. Wouldn't a few more mean less effort?"

Macro shrugged. "Slaves cost money. And isn't hard work what they're for?"

Glaxus decided to say no more. Macro was his friend and was possibly facing great jeopardy for him. Besides, such was the common attitude toward slavery throughout the empire. Free citizens virtually never challenged it as immoral because it made their lives easier. Indeed, half the population of the capitol was slaves. Like many soldiers, Glaxus had owned one himself. It was during his service in Egypt before he met Calvinia. A retiring centurion had given him a young Syrian, but he allowed the boy to escape after a few days. Owning another person had been an uncomfortable feeling, though he knew it was one most Romans didn't share. Calvinia was among the few he'd encountered who did. Telling her about it seemed to draw them closer together.

The Tiber was crowded with barges. Those being towed upstream kept near the east bank while those following the current to the sea stayed near the west. On both banks Glaxus saw that more estates had been built, though there were still plenty of little fruit and vegetable farms. It was mid-afternoon when they passed Rome's grain storehouses and moored at the wharves of the Emporium district. After giving the chief slave final instructions for delivering the marble, Macro led Glaxus up the nearest street.

The Emporium was as busy and clamorous as Glaxus recalled. The narrow, dirty byways rang with the sounds and voices of labor. Pounding, sawing, grinding, and shouting came from everywhere. Shifting breezes filled his nostrils first with the stench of tanneries and next with the rich smell of bakeries. Owners of cook shops bellowed for customers while olive oil sellers bargained loudly with buyers. Having been born into a very different social status, how could Calvinia be at home here? Members of the senatorial class usually disdained manual work. Though she undoubtedly told herself she wasn't an elitist, Glaxus was sure it couldn't have been an easy adjustment for her.

"Via Mercurius," said Macro, and took Glaxus along a side street lined with high insulae. Here there were men calling from windows, children writing on walls with chalk, women gossiping around public fountains. More shops were here also, and near the street's end Macro finally pointed to one. It was as small as Glaxus expected, squeezed in tightly between a busy wine seller and a bakery. Though its shutters were raised, Calvinia was nowhere in sight.

"Go on over. I'll wait at the cook shop on this side and keep my eye open."

Glaxus patted Macro's arm. "Be sure it's your real one."

The lone customer before Calvinia's shop was a girl holding a plucked chicken. She was about fourteen, with slender arms extending from her tunic and rings on every finger. Deciding it was wiser to wait until she left, Glaxus reluctantly mingled with the crowd gathered at the wine seller.

The girl leaned over the counter and looked down behind it as she spoke. "What is it, Calvinia? More pig's blood on the floor?"

"Yes. I must get it wiped up or I'll slip in it." The voice was as Glaxus remembered it, rich and resonant. "So Justina, does all go as planned?"

"Yes. I'll be a matrona when next you see me, with my own household to manage."

"And no more fetching chickens for your mother. May your ancestors and household gods bring you luck."

"You've never been married?"

"Yes, several years ago. He died."

"He was your first husband and chosen by your father?"

"He was."

"Then you've been free to choose your next husband yourself. Why haven't you?"

"There is one I would have chosen, but he was likely killed in the Germanic massacre."

"Oh Calvinia, I'm sorry. Perhaps there is another you might choose."

At this, Glaxus was glad to hear a deep sigh from behind the counter. "No. I think not."

Justina slung the chicken over her shoulder. "Well, I must get this bird home to mother. May you be granted prosperity."

"And you. Come see me again after your wedding."

When the girl was gone, Glaxus quickly strode over from the wine shop. "Calvinia!"

She stood up, her dark eyes widening at the sight of him. "Glaxus?" She had to lean against a wall to steady herself. "Glaxus! The gods have brought you home alive!"

"They have!" He rushed around the counter and hugged her close. "Though there were so many times I was sure it couldn't happen!"

"When I heard of the massacre, I gave up hope!"

"I received your letter at Fort Vetera, but it was lost with the rest of my possessions when we were attacked."

"That doesn't matter. It served its purpose. Your reply arrived by mail after Macro brought me the copy you gave him. I was pleased to know you still felt as I hoped you did. But then came news of the disaster and hearts all over Rome sank like stones, mine among them."

"You were correct in your letter, Calvinia. Varus had no military ability. He got thirty thousand people killed. His evil and stupidity haunt us even now."

"How do you mean?"

"There is much I must tell you. Can you close for the day?"

"Yes, immediately."

Calvinia lowered the shutters over the shop's front and lit an oil lamp. Glaxus watched her intently. Her black hair was parted down the middle and tied into a bun at the back. There were a few more wrinkles around her eyes, but her figure was still trim and her arms firm. Her white tunic was smeared with blood. She had apparently overcome any patrician reluctance to soil herself with work.

They sat under the lamp on stools as Glaxus once again related the tale. He concluded with his hope that Calvinia would be his mater familias and that they would adopt Hilda.

"Of course I'll be your wife, Glaxus, and the girl will be the child we couldn't have ourselves. But first we must face the situation before us. Do you think Pindocles is in Rome yet?"

"I would doubt it, but after giving the pouch to the Prefect, I intend to look for him anyway."

"You said his letter told you to seek him among the Greeks. I know many of them and speak Greek fluently, so it will be helpful if I come along."

"Absolutely not."

"Listen to me. I also know Cornelius' family. His stepsister and I were friends prior to my father's disgrace. Before the massacre she secretly came here twice to see me. She has long despised Cornelius because he and his younger brother once molested her slave girl."

Glaxus was certain such knowledge of the senatorial class would be useful now that he found himself pitted against them. Calvinia had also met the Emperor more than once. However, putting her in peril was unthinkable. "No. The risk is too great. Macro has joined me. He and I will deal with it."

"I insist, Glaxus. You can't expect me to just wait again while wondering if you've been killed." She stood up and folded her arms. "I must come."

He stood as well and took her by the shoulders. His feelings for her were even more intense than he thought they'd be. It appalled him to endanger her, but he knew she was right.

"Macro is keeping watch outside, Calvinia. Come with us."

She hurried to the stairs at the back of the shop. "Let me rinse off and put on a fresh tunic and a cloak."

Glaxus couldn't help thinking that Rome might be the Teutoburg hills this time, with Augustus as the marsh and Cornelius in the role of Herman. If he failed to kill Glaxus and retrieve the pouch before it was delivered, then his plan might be to trap his enemy in a vulnerable situation. In that case, he'd be counting on the Emperor to automatically side with a patrician against a plebeian. But perhaps Augustus' first duty would be to the empire as a whole, as Lucius said. And unlike the massacre, there was help on the way, if Pindocles arrived soon enough.

Calvinia came down in a dark tunic and hooded gray cloak. Hoping she wouldn't regret this decision, Glaxus led her into the street.

X

"Greetings, Macro," said Calvinia as he crossed over to meet them. "Your loyalty does us honor."

"Glaxus would do no less for me." He glanced at her cloak. "You're coming with us?"

"Yes. Glaxus has told me of the risk, but I will accept it."

"As you wish. So where do we go? To the Emperor's home? That's where the Praetorian Prefect is most likely to be this time of day."

Augustus' modest house on the Palatine Hill was essentially the hub of the Roman world. Glaxus had seen it only from a distance, never having had a reason to go near it until now. "Yes," he said. "To the Emperor's home."

Though as they walked, he found himself remembering Varus. The General had never seriously considered what actions the opposition might take. "Macro, what do you think Cornelius will do? Won't he suspect I'll go to the Palatine?"

"Probably. He may even use his family's wealth in an attempt to bribe the Prefect, though I think that unlikely."

"So do I." Calvinia was walking between them. "Seius Strabo is an ambitious man who knows fierce loyalty to the Emperor is his best means of advancement. He'd never accept a bribe."

"Then Cornelius will want to kill me before I reach Strabo, but to plan that he'd have to know I'm in Rome. Also, he'd need to accompany any assassins he hired because only he could recognize me on sight. That would be dangerous for him."

"Agreed," said Macro. "For those reasons I think we can safely go straight to the Palatine."

"Can we? Glaxus, when you sailed down from Cemenelum did you give your real name to the ship's captain?"

Glaxus saw where Calvinia was leading and instantly felt like a fool. "Yes, I wrote it in the manifest."

"Cornelius has many contacts and a great deal of money," she continued. "He could easily have every captain arriving in Ostia questioned about you. We should assume that he knows you're here and has put certain procedures in place around the Emperor's home."

Glaxus understood. "Though Prefect Strabo can't be bribed, several slaves and assistants working in Augustus' house can be."

"Can be and doubtlessly have been. After killing you, they'd take the pouch to Cornelius. Neither the Prefect nor the Emperor would ever know you were there."

"They couldn't help knowing he was there," said Macro. "Killing a man is a loud, bloody business."

"It is with swords and daggers," replied Calvinia, "but among the patricians of Rome the weapon of choice is poison. Glaxus would be offered a cup of wine by the bribed aides as soon as he revealed his identity."

"I'll give them a false name, as I should have done on the ship."

"They've surely been told to look for a tall centurion who might use an assumed name. You'd be suspected from the very moment they saw you. If you refused the wine, they would resort to more violent means. You might be asked to wait in a side chamber and then strangled. It's not as easy or convenient as poison, but it's silent and bloodless."

"I can prevent that by not entering any such chamber and by keeping Macro with me."

"Then you'll be told the Prefect will be unavailable all day and to leave the pouch for him, which you won't do. You'd have to leave the Palatine with it still in your possession. Several of Cornelius' henchmen would then know what you look like, making it easy for them to follow you. They'd kill you at their first opportunity and take the pouch. You could try bringing it to Prefect Strabo's home, but his slaves and aides will also be subject to bribing. The end results would be the same."

Glaxus stopped walking and pulled his companions close to a wall. "All right. We won't go to the Prefect now. Besides, we don't yet have what Pindocles is bringing. If we could present that to Strabo at the same time we give him the pouch, the evidence against Cornelius would be immediately overwhelming."

"But we'll still have to find our way through to the Prefect eventually," said Macro. "Or get someone to do it for us. Someone Cornelius and his myrmidons wouldn't suspect."

Glaxus became nervous as he watched Calvinia think about this. "Yes," she whispered. "Someone." Then she looked up at him. "But that's not a concern at the moment. Cornelius' henchmen can't follow us because they don't know who we are. Let's take advantage of that by searching for Pindocles."

"I was thinking the same, but where do we begin? He wrote that I should look for him in Rome among his fellow Greeks, but he didn't tell me who. He probably didn't want to be specific for fear his letter might have been intercepted."

"The Athenian philosophers," said Calvinia. "We went to see them in the old forum last time you were here, Glaxus. No Greek arrives, departs, or does anything in Rome without their knowing of it. If Pindocles has reached the city, they'll be able to tell us where he is."

"Able is one thing," observed Macro. "Willing is another."

"I've known most of them since I was a child. They'll confide in me if I explain to them in Greek why we need the information. We can also show them Pindocles' letter."

"Will they be in the old forum now?" Glaxus asked.

"They should be. In the mornings they earn their livings by teaching Latin rhetoric to the sons of Roman nobles, but in the afternoons they gather in the forum near the Basilica Julia. There they can observe the passing scene while conversing in their own language."

"Very well," said Glaxus. "To the philosophers." As they resumed walking, he began considering what to do if the old Greeks told them Pindocles hadn't arrived yet. Since that was most likely the case, another option would be needed.

Leaving the Emporium and entering the Aventine district, they went along the Vicus Armilustri toward the Circus Maximus. All was quiet around it, so there were obviously no chariot races being held. Glaxus was glad of that. They wouldn't have to work their way through the turbulent crowds that race days brought to the Circus. After passing it, they started up the Vicus Tuscus, the street that entered the old forum from this precinct. The smell of the cattle market on the left made him recall why he avoided this area as a boy.

Calvinia noticed him grimacing. "I go there almost every day to buy beef for my shop. You get used to the odor."

He pinched his nostrils shut and just nodded at her.

Passing between the temple of Castor and Pollux on the right and the Basilica Julia on the left, they entered the old forum. Glaxus knew its afternoons never matched its mornings for activity, but he thought the place busy enough. In front of Julius Caesar's temple merchants were selling vegetables and fruit from wooden stalls. Elsewhere, knots of people stood about in conversation. Visitors could be easily identified by how they gazed upon the huge buildings and pointed at the statues of Roman heroes.

The cold, gray day didn't diminish the sense of grandeur Glaxus always felt when he came here. He'd seen the pyramids during his tour of duty in Egypt and thought them merely huge piles of rock. In contrast, the Forum Romanum was a celebration of architectural order, beauty, and craftsmanship. Surely it would be standing long after the pyramids had crumbled.

Turning left, Calvinia led her two companions alongside the Basilica Julia. From within came the sound of courtrooms in session as lawyers tried to shout their way to victory. On the basilica's long front steps dozens of young men had chalked out game squares and avidly played at dice. It was also here that the white boards of the Acta Diurna were set up. Several slaves with tablets stood making copies for their masters.

Macro stopped. "Wait a moment. Let's have a look at the Daily Doings."

"It's just the usual gossip." Calvinia surveyed the boards. "I see that lecherous dog Hyboreas is marrying again. I hope this one takes everything he has."

Glaxus smiled, remembering his fears concerning Hyboreas and Calvinia.

Macro aimed his eye at the Doings and grunted. "The Emperor is still upset that so few are registering for the emergency army units. It says here he may start ordering executions for those not signing up."

"Using fear to control people is barbaric!" snapped Calvinia.

Macro shrugged. "Of course it is. That's why it works. Ask anyone who's been in the army. Tomorrow there will be a rise in the number of registrations. Wait and see."

Glaxus nudged Calvinia with his elbow. "Someday I must tell you about the realities of military life."

She suddenly seemed chastened. "I know. My childhood of wealth and privilege was ensured by soldiers like you and Macro, risking your lives on distant frontiers and doing what you were told. Without the army and its discipline the empire wouldn't exist."

"Perhaps one day the world won't need armies," said Macro, "but we shouldn't hold our breath." He reached out and tapped the nearest board. "See there, Glaxus. Cornelius' father, Senator Tydus Tulvis, has recently purchased a gladiator school. That could be bad news for us, because if I were Cornelius . . ."

". . . you'd consider getting some of your father's enslaved gladiators to do your dirty work." Glaxus was sure men who killed in the arena would kill anywhere, especially if promised their freedom. "You're right," he told Macro. "That's the sort of thing to expect from Cornelius and we must bear it in mind. Calvinia, do you see the philosophers?"

"Yes. At the far corner of the basilica, down by Saturn's temple."

The half-dozen Greeks were mostly bearded men of sixty or older, their sleek heads nodding and shaking vigorously during their discussion. Occasionally, one would tug on another's toga to emphasize a point. Glaxus watched in amusement as they fell silent when a slim young woman with a basket of fruit walked by. Studying her figure till she passed out of sight, they then resumed arguing.

As Calvinia approached, they hailed her in Greek and quickly gathered around her. She spoke to them in the same tongue, her voice low but intense. They questioned her for several minutes before she gestured at Glaxus and Macro to come over.

Once in the circle of Greeks, Glaxus was addressed in Latin by the oldest, a man of about seventy. His bald skull was ringed with wispy white hair and a beard of the same color curled around his purple lips. Glaxus vaguely remembered him.

"You are the soldier who accompanied Calvinia on one of her visits to us last year. Now you are to marry her?"

"Yes."

"I hope she has chosen well."

Glaxus was taken aback by this. Calvinia watched him nervously while the Greeks quietly waited.

"I can answer only for my own choices." He took her hand in his. "And I can assure you I have chosen well."

She smiled as the elder Greek laughed and clapped Glaxus on the shoulder. "Forgive a philosopher's little games, my friend. My name is Ametheos. Calvinia tells me you have survived the great massacre in Germania and now face related trouble here in Rome. We may be of assistance. However, before anyone says anything more, we'd like to read the physician's letter and the other documents you carry."

Glaxus let them do so, then promptly returned the tablets and birchbark to the pouch. "What can you tell me?"

"Pindocles is a man of judicious character," Ametheos answered. "He was right to warn you. Xenocratis here teaches rhetoric to

Falco, the younger brother of Cornelius, and has recently overheard them and their father speak of you by name. They have bribed several slaves at the homes of the Emperor and Prefect and have poison wine waiting for you, just as Calvinia guessed. Though we have known for a week this was being plotted, the name Glaxus meant nothing to us because neither you nor her mentioned it during that visit last year. Nor has she discussed her relationship with you in any of our conversations since then. She has always been very private, even as a child. Thus we couldn't know that Cornelius' plot would be of concern to her. We thought it just more intrigue involving the patrician families and their constant scramble for position and favor. Such matters are normally none of our business and best not interfered with."

"Then Pindocles isn't in Rome yet," Glaxus realized.

"No. My friendship with him goes back many years both here and in Greece. He'd have contacted me upon his arrival and informed us of your situation."

"We must find him, Ametheos," said Calvinia. "And soon."

"Which is why I think it inadvisable for you to simply stay in Rome and wait for him."

Glaxus knew what the old scholar meant, having reached the same conclusion. "You believe we should head up the Via Flaminia toward Ancona and intercept the doctor before he even enters the city."

"Yes. Make use of the fact that your enemies don't know he carries the incriminating tablet. Meeting him outside Rome would also be safer."

"Won't such a journey have to wait until tomorrow?" asked the Greek next to Ametheos. He was the only beardless one among them and also the youngest, appearing to be about fifty. He hadn't spoken in Latin until now. "The day grows late and I own an insula where they may stay tonight at no charge. They can start for Ancona in the morning when they're rested."

"Trion is right," said Ametheos. "Tomorrow at dawn is the best time to begin."

"Agreed." Glaxus turned to Trion. "If you'll show us to your insula, we'll—"

"Wait, Glaxus." Macro broke his silence. "We appreciate the offer, Ametheos, but I think it best that we stay tonight in a place of our own choosing. What you and your friends don't know, you can't divulge, even by accident."

"Your comrade speaks wisely. You cannot be too cautious." Ametheos pointed toward the center of the forum. "Lose yourselves in the crowd and we will remember nothing of this meeting."

But Glaxus wanted to thank him first. "You're help has been tremendous. Now we don't need to guess about Cornelius' strategy."

Calvinia grasped Ametheos' hands. "We owe you much, my friend. We'll come see you again when this is over."

"Then may it be over soon." The wrinkles around the Greek's gray eyes deepened as he smiled at her. "This is the daughter the gods should have given me," he told Glaxus. "Can you understand?"

Glaxus thought of Hilda. "Yes, I can."

Ametheos nodded. "Now you must go, and be watchful with every step. Rome is a city of schemes and schemers. There could be people and motives at work here of which we know nothing."

As they fell in with the throngs walking toward Argiletum Street, Glaxus suggested they make for the Subura district. "It's the pigsty of the city, but we'll find lodging there with little trouble."

Leaving the old forum, they made their way between the senate house and the Basilica Amelia. Beyond these on the left were the newer forums of Julius Caesar and Augustus, which Glaxus considered much less splendid. After passing the forums, they entered the booksellers' district. Heaps of scrolls lay on tables outside the shops as the proprietors advertised their wares at full voice.

"Herodotus! Thucydides! Sallust! The works of these great historians for only eight denarii!"

"Caesar's account of his wars in Gaul! Learn of the enemy we now face again! Fifteen denarii! Cheaper than cheap!"

"The glory of Roman poetry! Virgil! Horace! Catullus! Yours for merely ten denarii! Hurry, hurry!"

"Books!" snarled Macro. "A waste of time and money! For entertainment there are the gladiator games, chariot races, and theatres. Why should people strain their minds with a book?"

Calvinia erupted in laughter. "And perhaps someday, Macro, there will be a means of bringing the games, races, and theatre into your very home! Then you may sit, eat, and watch while straining neither your body nor your mind."

"Mock me if you like, Calvinia, but I speak for more citizens than you know."

"Enough," said Glaxus. "We must soon find an insula."

The poverty and decay of the Subura was as bad as Glaxus anticipated. He'd passed through this part of Rome only twice before, usually going out of his way to avoid it. The insulae here were the worst of the worst; creaking, groaning wrecks begging to burn. The place they finally chose was across the street from a pile of smoldering ruins. A couple of boys told them an insula was destroyed early that morning. The City Watch came with buckets and pumps to keep the fire from spreading, but a family on the top floor had died. This in mind, Glaxus decided the three of them would stay on the ground floor and in one room.

"It will be safer that way," he explained. "We'll each take turns staying awake while the other two sleep. If there's a fire, we can be out in the street in an instant. Keeping someone awake also affords protection against surprise attack."

Macro betrayed no discomfort at this arrangement, though Calvinia blushed as they were met by the hoarse old woman who owned the building.

"You and two men?" she croaked. "In the same room?"

Glaxus intervened, holding out three aurei. "One of these for each of us, matrona, and no more questions. Done?"

"Done." Her gnarly fingers tightened around the coins and she pointed down the hall. "Fourth door on the left. The common latrine is under the stairs and has plenty of sponges and small sticks. Be gone at sunrise."

They slept on the pair of rickety cots fully clothed, with Glaxus taking the last watch. He wanted to remove his toga and especially the ring-mail under it, but he did neither. As a young legionary, he once had to wear his armor for an entire week. He hoped that wouldn't be necessary now, but who could say what awaited them? When he glanced out the window and saw the faintest glow in the east, he awakened his companions and they were on their way. Stopping briefly at a cook shop for food, they made toward the Via Flaminia and began following it north through the central shopping district. As usual, all Rome was up early, so the streets were alive with people.

Glaxus was eager to get out of the teeming city because wagons were prohibited only within its limits. Once in the country they would be able to rent one. He asked Calvinia about this.

"Yes, there will be horses and wagons for hire just north of the city. We should be able to get a four-wheeled raeda."

"Good. That's what we'll do." With Macro walking a few steps ahead of them, Glaxus pulled her close. "I wish this were finished."

"So do I, but we can't think of ourselves now. Cornelius must be exposed and brought down. He knows he could never succeed Augustus, but he's still young. He'll undoubtedly plot to succeed Tiberius, who is already fifty-one and not yet Emperor. Though to have any hope of that he must prevent his reply to your message from being seen by Augustus. How do you think he explained his survival at the massacre?"

"Undoubtedly by lying about his valor. Of course, his fellow patricians will be eager to believe him since he's one of their own. Without proof, they'll doubt anything I say against him because I'm a low-born plebeian." Glaxus remembered Lucius' warning about this. "We must find the physician, Calvinia, and recover that tablet."

"Judging from Pindocles' letter and from what you've told me of him, he clearly comprehends the situation. Don't you think he'll take measures to protect himself and safely deliver the tablet to you?"

"Definitely," agreed Glaxus, but had no idea what those measures would be. The crafty Greek could be counted on not to do the expected.

They were nearing the Campus Agrippae. With stately homes on both sides of the street, this district was the very opposite of the Subura. Many senatorial families lived here, so Glaxus asked Calvinia if there was any risk of encountering Cornelius or someone from his clan.

"I wouldn't think so. They have their mansions on the Esquiline. It's unlikely they'd be in this part of the city so early in the day."

Macro slowed down to let Glaxus and Calvinia join him. "Look there," he said. "Clients."

In front of every home was a gathering of citizens, mostly men. Tucking their togas into place and rubbing the sleep from their eyes, they rudely jostled each other for a spot near the door. The few women among them were no less aggressive.

"Parasites!" snapped Macro. "Allergic to work!"

Though he shared Macro's sentiments, Glaxus said nothing. His mother's brother had been a client. Patronage from patricians was an old custom which most plebeian Romans now considered a right, like the bread dole. If Augustus ever banned one or both, it could ignite a rebellion.

At the mansion they were passing, an elderly slave opened the door, then was nearly run down when the clients rushed into the vestibule. Those at the next house had already received their money and been released by their patron. They hurriedly brushed past Macro, one taking a healthy shove from him for getting too close. Across the street, still others counted their coins as they filed out. Instead of scurrying away, this group stood around morosely in front of the entrance.

"Their patron hasn't released them," remarked Macro. "Now they'll have to follow his litter into the forum and kiss his rump all day. Why don't the leeches find employment?"

That Rome was full of idlers and shirkers was no secret. Glaxus didn't see how Augustus could be surprised at the difficulty of recruiting men for the emergency forces. Why work or risk your life when someone was willing to fill your stomach and your pocket in exchange for nothing?

Despite the cool air, people swarmed over the Campus Agrippae as well as the nearby Campus Martius. Some rode horses on the vast lawns while others wrestled or ran footraces. Trios of children played triangle ball under the trees. Glaxus had played the same game here as a boy when there were fewer structures in the area. Now the low hills were dotted with theatres, statues, and temples. Glancing over his left shoulder, he could see the shrine to all the gods, the Pantheon. Crowds had already begun pouring into it to make offerings and petitions.

At mid-morning they reached an inn outside the city where they could hire a raeda and two horses. Calvinia suggested they buy some bread and dried fruit from the innkeeper, along with a few jugs of water. When they were ready, she sat between Glaxus and Macro and volunteered to take the reins first.

Like all the empire's highways, the Via Flaminia had been solidly built and its stone surface maintained with care. The wagon rolled over it loudly, but smoothly. Farms and orchards stretched into the distance on both sides while boys tending flocks of sheep waved at them as they passed. The November sky was clear, yet the sun didn't feel warm on Glaxus' face. As the day waned, he carefully observed every fellow traveler they met heading the opposite way. Some were on foot or horseback, though most rode in wagons or chariots. He hoped the doctor could be intercepted on the road, and soon. Going all the way to Ancona would mean having to cross the Apennine Mountains in snow season.

The shadows were long when they came upon an inn at the twentieth milestone. The fading sign above the door proclaimed it the "Inn of Mercury and Neptune." Single-story and built of stone, it was set against a hillside covered with pine trees and thick brush. There were already several wagons in front. The boy who came out to take their horses to the stable told them rooms were still available.

Glaxus decided the safest arrangement would be the same as last night's. "Macro, you'll take the first watch this time, then I, then Calvinia. We mustn't drop our guard for a moment."

Inside, smoke from the fireplace filled the dining hall where a varied collection of travelers sat eating, swearing, and playing dice. Glaxus was sure so coarse a group would laugh out loud when the three of them asked for one room. Attracting attention was dangerous, but here it seemed unavoidable.

The owner was a lean, dark-eyed man of middle age. He quickly looked them over, clearly trying to guess what they could afford to pay. Glaxus learned long ago this was common practice among innkeepers. Customers who appeared indigent might be turned away altogether.

The man's gaze lingered on Calvinia. Even in drab clothing, her countenance and bearing plainly revealed she was no plebeian. He rubbed his dirty hands together and smiled. "Four aurei apiece for the night, my friends. Two rooms or three, however you please."

Glaxus thought this price outrageous, but before he could speak, one of the dice players shouted, "Opportunist! You only charged me two denarii!"

"Two?" cried someone else. "The skinny rascal charged me five!"

"Do you hear that?" Macro shook his finger under the man's nose. "You're a thief and the son of a thief! Now give us one of your filthy rooms and make it a total of nine denarii!"

"The three of you in a single room?"

"Yes! Why should I let my cousins fatten your account by taking separate rooms?" Macro thrust four coins into the man's hand. "Five more when we leave! Now lead us there and bring food and hot wine!"

A cheer went up as the innkeeper shuffled backward. "Yes sir! This way!"

The room was indeed filthy. Scraps of food lay strewn on the floor and the ceiling was stained with soot from oil lamps. A fresco on one of the walls depicted crude images of Mercury and Neptune, the guardian deities of the inn. Glaxus barred the door as Calvinia closed and latched the window shutters. She then scrutinized the room's two cots and slapped her palms onto the blankets. Fleas by the dozens were sent hopping into the air.

Macro laughed and poured out three cups of steaming wine. "This is worse than where we stayed last night. When the fleas are finished with us, we'll have lost ten pounds each by morning." He sniffed at the cups. "I hope that scoundrel doesn't mix his wine with piss. My parents owned an inn for a few years and to make the wine go further, they would—"

"Macro, please!" Calvinia took a cup. "Just let me drink it in blissful ignorance."

Glaxus also took one. "A clever diversion with the innkeeper. You spared Calvinia some embarrassment and kept us from being thought of suspiciously by the other lodgers."

"That was nothing." Macro bit off a piece of bread. "He needed to be put in his place, anyway. The empire is full of greedy dogs like him who worship profit above all else. I've been called such myself once or twice."

Calvinia was gingerly sipping from her cup. "Horace gave that advice years ago. 'Money is the first thing to seek,' he wrote. 'Virtue after money.' It's an attitude that will never change."

Macro shrugged. "Why should it? Virtue alone won't put a meal on your table."

"And money alone won't stop evil," countered Glaxus. "You're not helping us against Cornelius for money. You're a virtuous man whether you know it or not."

"Promise you won't tell anyone?"

"I promise. Now after we eat, you must begin your watch while Calvinia and I get some sleep."

When Macro roused him, Glaxus asked if anything had been stirring.

"Only what you usually hear in a place like this. Quarreling, carousing, gambling."

"I was too tired to care." Glaxus got up. "Now you must rest."

After Macro lay on the cot, Glaxus checked the crossbar on the door. He then touched the pitcher of wine and discovered it was still warm despite the cold air in the room. Another cupful would be welcome, but he refrained. He had to stay alert. Besides, he was bothered less by the cold than by the itching fleabites on his forearms.

A glowing shaft of light from a full moon stretched in between the window shutters, casting a small patch of brightness onto the floor. Glaxus happened to be glancing at this patch when it suddenly disappeared.

He drew his sword and rushed toward the window.

"Intruders!"

XI

The first man at the window was huge, easily breaking open the shutters with his arms. He had one muscular leg in the room by the time Glaxus reached him.

Striking the initial blow was vital. Glaxus went low, driving the sword through that big thigh and into the wall. The trespasser screamed and dropped a dagger he was wielding. Wrenching the sword free, Glaxus put the finishing thrust into the man's mouth and out the top of his head.

Attempting to shove the body through the window, Glaxus saw two more men appear and push it back in, sending him sprawling on the floor under it. Macro and Calvinia were on their feet by now and under immediate assault. One of the attackers forced Macro away from the window with a three-pointed lance, thereby gaining entrance to the room.

A trident was a gladiator's weapon! Macro had been right. Cornelius had hired them from his father's school.

Retreating with sword in hand, Macro desperately parried his opponent's thrusts. When Calvinia stepped in front of the window and behind the gladiator, Glaxus panicked.

"No, Calvinia!" He struggled frantically to heave off the corpse. "Get to the door! Get out!"

Ignoring him, she seized the rear of the trident's handle and pushed down, forcing its head upward. Now able to slip under the three prongs, Macro did so while stabbing out hard and straight. Bloody intestines smeared the floor as the gladiator moaned and collapsed. Glaxus was pleased the arrogant fools had worn only their loincloths and no armor. He was also relieved Calvinia's courage hadn't gotten her hurt. With a firm effort, he finally pushed away the body of the first attacker and threw it over by that of the second.

But hadn't there been at least three of them?

"Calvinia! Move away from the window!"

She hardly had time to budge before a hairy pair of hands reached in and grasped her under the arms.

"Glaxus!"

Her scream impaled him like a spear. He leaped to his feet and dashed forward, but she was instantly pulled out of the room.

Macro reached the window first. "She's being carried to the wagon yard out front!"

Glaxus caught a glimpse of a shadow slipping around a corner of the inn. He began to climb through, but Macro held him back.

"No, Glaxus! The undergrowth is dense. There could be any number of them waiting for us."

"You in there!" The voice was deep but cold. "The Centurion and his friend. Our proposition is simple. Come out to the wagon yard and give us the documents you carry. We'll then release the woman. Delay and she will be killed."

Glaxus knew he had to try a ruse of some kind. "I must come out alone. When your comrades met their end, they took my friend with them."

"He swings a quick sword for a dead man. If you think he can take us by surprise while you negotiate, you're mistaken. You must both come to the wagon yard now and you must be unarmed."

"The other lodgers will be roused and you'll be outnumbered."

The deep voice laughed. "Do you believe they'll risk their lives in the dark for a stranger? They're cowering in their beds even now."

That had to be true. Glaxus was sure the combat awakened the entire inn, but no one had pounded on the door. "All right!" He ripped off his bloody toga. "We're coming out! But by all the gods, you'd better not harm her!"

"You're in no position to make threats. Come out now."

Macro tossed away his sword and removed his toga. "They have no intention of making a trade. Cornelius has certainly instructed them to kill us all."

"Without a doubt," agreed Glaxus. "They must have been waiting in the undergrowth near the inn and saw us arriving. They also saw Calvinia closing the shutters and that's how they knew what room we were in. But how did they know our plans, and if Cornelius isn't with them, how did they recognize me?" He saw just one answer. "Aside from we three, only the Greeks knew we were heading to Ancona to meet Pindocles. One of them went to Cornelius."

"But which one," asked Macro, "and why?"

"I don't know why, but I think I know which. There was a beardless one named Trion who offered to let us stay in his insula. He wanted to be sure we remained in the city and in a location he knew while he informed Cornelius about us."

"Then if we had stayed there, Cornelius would have had us attacked last night."

"Without a doubt. You were wise to insist we stay elsewhere, Macro. So instead, Cornelius sent Trion along with some gladiators to intercept us on the road to Ancona. They must have left Rome an hour or two before us, knowing we'd have to stop here for the night."

"We grow tired of waiting, Centurion! Come out!"

"Glaxus!" Calvinia's voice called loudly. "There are six of them left! They—"

Then silence.

"We're coming! Don't harm her!" Glaxus used his sword to pry loose a floorboard. He stuffed the leather pouch under it and stamped it back into place. "We'll attempt to deal with them. We'll say that if they release her to us we'll tell them where the pouch is hidden."

"The odds are all on their side," said Macro.

"I know, but we must try." Reluctantly laying aside his sword and dagger, Glaxus noticed something gleaming on the moonlit floor. It was the arena-style dagger dropped by the first gladiator. Not being as large as the military type, it would have a certain advantage. He snatched it up and handed it to Macro. "Slip this under your ring mail. We won't be completely helpless."

"You should take it, Glaxus."

"No. I want you to have it. You're already risking so much for me. I won't go out there with a weapon while you have none." As he unbarred the door and swung it open, Glaxus tried to resist a growing sense of despair.

The hallway was dark and quiet. He thought about knocking on a door and asking for help, but knew it would be useless. Fighting was common in country inns. No one would concern themselves with another's conflict. Besides, showing up with several men might get Calvinia killed immediately.

The dining hall where they had met the inn's proprietor was deserted. After slowly opening the door to the wagon yard, Glaxus shouted into the night. "I don't have the documents on me! They're in a pouch which I've hidden in the inn. You must release the woman first, then after one of you accompanies us back to the city, I will tell him where it is."

"You're trying to stall us." The deep voice was alarmingly close. "Tell us now or we kill her."

"How do I know that when you have it, you won't kill all three of us?"

"What's to stop us from doing that first and then burning this place to the ground? We prefer to retrieve the documents, but their destruction will accomplish our purpose."

"In that case, why should I give them to you? We know you've been ordered to kill us no matter what, so proceed and be done! We'll even make the job easy for you!" Glaxus strode angrily into the moonlit yard. The several wagons scattered around it were casting deep shadows on the dirt.

With Macro beside him, he walked to the largest clear spot. No one was visible. Calvinia had shouted that there were six of them. Perhaps six was all she saw. There could be a dozen or more hiding in the yard.

"Well?" demanded Glaxus. "Here we are! Kill us! Or if you're truly gladiators, give me a gladiator's chance! Hand me a sword and let me fight one of you to determine the outcome!"

The deep voice laughed. "If you won, the rest of us would have to return empty-handed and we'd be executed on the spot. You're courage and determination are commendable, but you're right. Cornelius has told us to kill you all. After that, we'll be freed."

A man at least a span taller than Glaxus stepped from behind the nearest wagon. With his left arm around her waist, he easily held Calvinia off the ground. She was limp, groaning softly as blood oozed from a wound on her forehead. The giant kept the tip of his sword just below her chin. Glaxus instinctively took a step forward, but stopped when Macro whispered sharply.

"Pointless, Glaxus. We must wait and hope the gods turn things in our favor. When they attack us, I'll try to kill one and get his weapon to you."

But how would that help Calvinia? Glaxus racked his mind for a way that would at least give her a chance.

The giant spoke next, revealing that his was the deep voice. "It's a shame to butcher you two like sheep. You would have had fine careers as gladiators. Your woman also has spirit, Centurion." He turned, revealing a long, thin gash down the back of his sword arm. "She pulled a meat cleaver from beneath her cloak and tried to carve me like a goose."

Glaxus realized she must have slipped it under her clothes before they left her shop, probably when she went upstairs to change. Too bad she couldn't have reached the giant's throat with it. Celtic from the look of him, he too was wearing only a red loincloth and sandals. The scars of many combats marked his massive upper body. His sword was of the cavalry type, its blade considerably longer than that used by foot soldiers. To his right, five more men with similar weapons appeared from behind wagons.

Calvinia had been correct. There were six of them remaining, but one was not a gladiator.

Glaxus felt no surprise at seeing that the sixth man was Trion.

"You Greek snake!" Macro bellowed. "If I cross the Styx tonight, I'm dragging you with me!"

Trion ignored Macro and spoke to the giant. "The time has come, Pugnax. We can search their room afterwards and burn the inn if necessary."

"And then what?" demanded Glaxus. "On to Ancona to intercept Pindocles and kill him as well?"

"Yes. Though the doctor is no enemy of mine, he must die with you because he bars the path of Cornelius, who seeks to be emperor after Tiberius. If Cornelius gains ultimate power, he will need a tutor to any sons he may have. He has promised me that position in exchange for my help. As tutor to future emperors, I could shape history for years to come, as Aristotle did with Alexander the Great."

Glaxus recalled his conversation with Plutarius about Alexander. The Chief Centurion had spoken of each Roman needing to subordinate uniqueness for the good of the empire. If Cornelius and Trion achieved power, they would do exactly the reverse. They would subordinate the good of the empire to assert their own personalities. How long could any society last under the rule of such men? Glaxus realized something was at stake here far beyond the lives of three people.

Trion turned to Pugnax again. "Now!"

The giant nodded at his four colleagues and they sauntered forward, obviously expecting little resistance. Each was nearly the size of the giant and as badly scarred. One had no nose.

Glaxus grabbed Macro and hugged him close. "Good-bye, my friend. At least we did our best." As they were chest to chest, Glaxus lowered his voice. "You must make a throw for the man holding Calvinia."

Macro eased the dagger from under his ring mail and into Glaxus' hand. "You do it. I can't aim as well with one eye."

"All right. Then we'll run among the wagons and hope the others follow us. Perhaps we can attack them from behind in the dark." Glaxus didn't have much hope for this plan, but couldn't see another.

The other gladiators were drawing near, so there was no time to waste. Estimating his distance from Pugnax at some five or six paces, Glaxus picked a spot in the middle of that huge torso. Spinning away from Macro, he threw the dagger with all the force he could muster.

But the giant reacted swiftly. Dropping Calvinia, he bent low and to his right as the dagger plunged into the wagon seat behind him. His comrades paused, apparently surprised that their victims were not helpless.

"Most resourceful, Centurion!" The giant raised his sword over Calvinia. "But that was your final cast of the dice! Kill them!"

Though certain he wouldn't reach her, Glaxus resolved to make a dash toward Calvinia. It was at this instant that he heard a familiar hiss.

Yes! The sound of arrows cutting through the air!

The giant was the first to be struck, in the very spot at which Glaxus had aimed the dagger. Reeling away from Calvinia, he collapsed onto his back as another shaft caught him in the neck.

The remaining gladiators tried to dive under the wagons, but didn't get far. Unarmored and without shields, all four were hit before moving half a step. The noseless one died last. As he fell face down, the arrows in his chest were driven out through his back.

Sprinting over to Calvinia, Glaxus gently stood her upright and examined her head wound. It was long and jagged, but not deep. It might have been done with the pommel of a sword.

"Calvinia! Can you hear me?"

She looked at him with unfocused eyes. "Glaxus! What—what happened? Are we safe?"

"Yes, but I don't yet know who helped us or why."

Considering the direction from which the arrows came and their angle of flight, Glaxus guessed the archers had been on the inn's roof. Glancing that way, he saw nothing, but could hear the scuffling of many feet. Perhaps their rescuers were coming down to show themselves.

Macro walked over to look at the giant's body. "I saw him in the arena a few times. He was called Pugnax the Ferocious. Five more victories and he'd have earned his freedom."

"That would have been five more chances to die," Glaxus said. "So he chose what he thought was an easier way out. If I were enslaved and forced to fight like an animal, I'm not sure I'd have done differently."

"Where's Trion's body?" asked Calvinia.

"There's an arrow in the ground where he was standing," noticed Macro, "but I see no blood. Whoever they were, they must have thought the gladiators were the most important targets and sent most of their arrows that way. Trion probably fled into the woods when he saw his cause was lost."

"He has nowhere to go." Calvinia was leaning against Glaxus, her voice sounding stronger. "If he returned to Rome now, Cornelius would have him killed for failing. His Greek comrades will offer him no help because he betrayed them as well as us. We'll report his actions to the Praetorian Prefect who will inform Augustus, then there won't be anywhere in the empire he can hide. He faces a situation worse than death and he surely knows it. He may simply kill himself."

"A pity," said Macro. "Scum like him would make good lion bait."

The door to the inn opened and several young men with bows came hustling out, led by the proprietor. "There's the trash that would have burned my business!" He kicked the body of the nearest gladiator. "The only burning they'll do will be in Hades!" He fixed his glare next on Macro. "See the trouble you bring upon me, you lying jackal! These two are no more your cousins than I am! I should have put an arrow straight through your ear!"

"Why didn't you?" asked Macro.

"Because you still owe me for the room!"

"Here." Macro took his money purse from beneath his armor and handed it to the innkeeper. "A hundred aurei."

"A hundred!" The man eagerly began counting the coins as the other archers crowded around him, their hands extended.

"Who are your companions?" Glaxus asked.

"My sons and nephews, if that's any of your concern."

"Well, I'd like to thank them and you for saving us."

"Bah! I was saving my livelihood! I heard the commotion in your room, but what's that to me? It was when I heard talk of setting fire to my inn that I awakened the boys and we grabbed our bows. I let an arrow fly at the older man in the tunic, but missed and didn't have any more to waste on him. After that, he disappeared among the trees." The innkeeper dropped the empty purse. "Now be off my property by dawn. I'll dump these five dogs into the cesspit later."

"There are more in our room," Macro informed him.

"The pit is deep enough for all. Just be gone before sunrise and I'll clean up the mess."

If the man overheard anything Trion said about Cornelius wanting to be Emperor, it plainly didn't interest him. And so the course of history had perhaps been changed because a citizen defended his source of income. As good a reason as any, decided Glaxus. "It's only a couple of hours before dawn, Macro. We may as well make ready to head for Ancona. Pindocles must still be found."

"As you say. I'll see to the horses and wagon."

"Come, Calvinia." Glaxus walked her slowly toward the inn. "Let's wash and bandage your wound."

The archers were already in the dining hall, boasting about their aim and the unexpected money they had earned. The proprietor's wife appeared and quickly confiscated his share of the coins. Glaxus took the opportunity to ask her for some hot water and clean cloth. Helping Calvinia to a bench, he carefully rinsed and bandaged the wound.

When this was done, he spoke softly. "I must go to the room and get the pouch. I hid it there."

She nodded slowly. "I'll be all right, Glaxus. My head isn't aching as much now. I can lie down in the back of the wagon when we're under way."

"Good. I won't be long."

Moonlight was still shining through the room's window, casting a soft glow over the bodies of the first two gladiators. Crouching, Glaxus picked up his sword and pried loose the floorboard. He then sheathed his weapon and reached down for the pouch.

By the sheerest of luck he had crouched over the board while facing the open door. When he saw Trion lunge from behind it, he was able to evade a sword slash by springing backward toward the window. Landing on his buttocks, he tried to stand, but stumbled over one of the bodies. Snatching up the trident, he jabbed the sharp points at his advancing enemy. Trion had to halt as Glaxus scrambled to his feet.

"You have failed in your mission and the gladiators are all dead! You must surrender!"

"I can't! Stand aside and let me have the pouch!"

Glaxus drew his sword and dropped the trident. "No!"

Trion circled toward the window. Glaxus countered by circling toward the door and stopping there. His opponent was at least ten years older and obviously had no combat training. A real warrior would have come from behind the door thrusting instead of slashing. If there was to be a fight, Glaxus was certain of the outcome.

Trion seemed to be also. He kept backing toward the window, his breathing quick and shallow as he held his sword out with two hands. Glaxus chose not to advance on him. "There's been enough violence. Come with us to the Praetorian Prefect and throw yourself upon the mercy of the Emperor. Confess your part in this and implicate Cornelius."

"I'll flee to Greece! There will be somewhere there I can avoid the Emperor's eye!"

"You won't even get aboard a ship. Think clearly. You must give up."

Plainly gripped with fear and indecision, Trion had retreated all the way to the window. "I'd be executed! Or you'll kill me right here!"

"I will not. I promise you." While saying this, Glaxus barely noticed something moving behind Trion. A piece of the darkness seemingly came to life and floated forward. Shapeless and silent, it swiftly approached the window. A dagger materialized from out of it and glinted in the moonlight over Trion's head. The blade came down with such momentum that both his hands were easily pierced, causing him to scream and drop his sword. Before he could even begin to struggle, the dagger was instantly pulled free and shifted to his throat. Once before, at Fort Aliso, Glaxus had seen someone blend into the night like this.

"Pindocles, don't! He can help us against Cornelius!"

Keeping the dagger point lodged in the hollow of Trion's throat, the physician pulled back his hood with his free hand. "Greetings, Centurion. The gods have graciously favored our efforts." He slipped a battered writing tablet from under his black robes and tossed it to Glaxus. "And they have brought the day of reckoning upon our enemies."

XII

Before they left the inn, Pindocles bandaged Trion's hands and sewed up Calvinia's head. Despite Trion's cries, Macro tightly bound his wrists, using the pain to make him reveal which wagon he and the gladiators had used. "I'll take this bastard in his own wagon, Glaxus. You lead the way in ours."

"Very good, but watch him closely."

"That I will."

By mid-afternoon, they were nearing Rome. Calvinia had slept awhile in the wagon's rear, but now she was sitting up front between Pindocles and Glaxus.

Glaxus still couldn't believe the story Pindocles told. He'd thought the Greek would do something unexpected to foil any pursuers, but this seemed extreme. "You walked across the Apennines without using the roads? And entirely at night?"

"Yes. My familiarity with the stars and the land enabled me to avoid the roads while walking across farms and through the mountains. I would sleep by day in the forest or in abandoned barns. It was difficult, but I deemed it necessary."

"And you were passing the inn when you heard the fighting?" said Calvinia.

"Indeed. I was walking along the wooded hilltop behind your room. As I drew closer, I also heard a woman shout the name Glaxus. By the time I was in position to see the wagon yard, the arrows were flying and Trion was slipping away. I followed and located him during his confrontation with the Centurion. I decided to intervene lest he flee through the window. I can assure you I had no intention of slitting his throat."

"If we hadn't been attacked by the gladiators," realized Glaxus, "we wouldn't have found you because of your evasive strategy."

"Then it would seem Cornelius has brought about that which he sought to prevent. The gods often make it so with wicked men."

"Do you know Trion well?" Glaxus asked.

"He is only an acquaintance whom I never affronted or felt affronted by. His designs against me must have been rooted in ambition, as he told you."

"We all need ambition to make something of ourselves," Calvinia remarked. "It's in knowing when to control it that so many of us fail."

Pindocles glanced at her, then addressed Glaxus. "I can see why you urgently wanted a tablet on which to write your letter to her. She has a keen mind and a strong character. She has also been highly blessed with that Mediterranean beauty for which the women of Italia are so justly famous, a beauty exceeded only by the women of Greece. Such a wife will keep you active in many ways, Centurion."

Pindocles then exchanged a few words in Greek with Calvinia. They looked at Glaxus and smiled, causing him to squirm on the wagon seat. He'd have to master that language someday.

Arriving at the inn from which they rented the wagon, they prepared to enter the city on foot. Glaxus donned his helmet and red cloak, and at Calvinia's urging pinned on his military decorations. "You're still in the army," she told him, "so wear these proudly. Doing so will impress the Prefect." Lastly, Glaxus took from his woolen bag the emblem of the 19th Legion and clasped it to his chest.

Trion spit onto the street and sneered. "The badge of a dead legion!"

Glaxus heard this and was instantly returned to his last stand at the Teutoburg hills. Once more the corpses of his comrades were scattered everywhere as the Gauls closed in on him. These images blurred and shifted, becoming the tent where he'd confronted Herman. Glaxus stared at Trion, but saw the arrogant face of the enemy chieftain. His sword was out before he knew what he was doing.

"You butchering Gaulish traitor! You'll brag less without your tongue!"

"Glaxus!" shouted Calvinia. "No!"

The sights and sounds of those incidents had overtaken his memory with no warning, but upon hearing Calvinia, he felt them fade as quickly as they came.

Pindocles gently returned Glaxus' sword to the sheath. "Calm yourself, Centurion. The traitor you speak of is not here, nor are those he butchered. You have seen horrors from the past suddenly conjured up by the actions of the present. I underwent a similar experience during my sea voyage to Ancona. Let us leave the dead to their rest. If they haunt us, it is by our choosing, not theirs. All they ask of us is justice, and that we will give them today."

Glaxus put one hand on Calvinia's shoulder and nodded at Pindocles. "You're a doctor of the soul as well as the body."

"I do what I can, when I can. That is all any physician may do." Pindocles then wagged a finger in front of Trion's pallid face and barked at him in Greek. Trion nodded hastily and said nothing more.

As they began walking south on the Via Flaminia, Macro mentioned the problem of getting through to the Prefect. "It's likely Cornelius still has people bribed and in position at Augustus' home, especially since he hasn't received word from his assassins."

Calvinia suddenly seized Glaxus' arm. "I know a way."

He remembered watching her ponder this problem yesterday and once again it made him nervous. "No, Calvinia. You won't be the one who goes to Prefect Strabo. The danger is too great. While betraying us to Cornelius, Trion certainly told him about you. It's just as certain that Cornelius then told the bribed slaves at the Emperor's house. You'd never get through. We must find someone we can trust and who they wouldn't suspect."

"I wasn't going to suggest myself. We can get Cornelius' stepsister to do it. You recall I told you how she has visited me twice at my shop and how she hates him."

"Enough to shame him and her family?" asked Pindocles.

"She wouldn't think of it as shaming her family, but as loyalty to the empire, and she'd be right. I've known Sylvia since she was born. When she learns Cornelius betrayed the Roman army, she won't hesitate to help us. Her betrothed was a tribune in the 19th who died in the massacre. She—"

"Wait, Calvinia." Glaxus saw in his mind the bleeding young man who had been sitting by Varus' chariot, mumbling the name Sylvia. "Was her betrothed a tribune called Decimus?"

"Yes! Did you know him?"

"None of that rank were friends of mine, but he told me how he was wounded in the marsh during the massacre and how Cornelius abandoned him. It's here in the tablets as I related it to Lucius at Fort Aliso."

"When Sylvia learns this," promised Calvinia, "she won't hesitate to help us."

"Do you know where she is now?" Macro asked.

"At this hour she's in the public baths of Agrippa with her friends."

Glaxus noticed they were near the Vipsanian Portico. Ahead and to the right was the Pantheon with the baths just beyond it. "She'll obviously be in the women's section, so only Calvinia can seek her, but I'll go along as far as the entrance."

"No, Glaxus. You'll draw too much attention in your uniform. I should do this alone."

Glaxus agreed. "Then we'll wait here, but you must hurry. If we arrive at the Palatine too late, the Prefect may be gone for the day and we'd have to come back tomorrow. By then, Cornelius might realize his gladiators have failed. We don't want to give him another night to recruit more of them for a second attempt."

"We won't arrive too late," Calvinia asserted. "I'll quickly find Sylvia."

"When you do," suggested Pindocles, "tell her who each of us is and how we're involved. She can then pass that information on to the Prefect."

"I'll tell her."

To Glaxus' relief, Calvinia returned in less than twenty minutes with a girl of about sixteen. Slim of body with high cheekbones, she wore a cloak and tunic similar to Calvinia's and was bedecked with expensive jewelry. Beneath her hood, Glaxus could see that her black hair was still damp. She padded lightly over the grass and straight up to him.

"My name is Sylvia. Calvinia says you were with my poor Decimus at the massacre. Did he die well?"

"Yes, and he died cursing Cornelius."

"Tell me what he said."

Glaxus did so, and also let her read the account of it in the tablets. "And now we ask you to help us get this information to the Praetorian Prefect who will give it to the Emperor. Your stepbrother will then have to answer for his deeds."

"Of course I'll help you. Did Calvinia tell you that Cornelius once forced himself upon my slave girl?"

"She told me."

"She also says he had that man with the bound hands lead a team of gladiators to kill you all." Sylvia threw back her hood and flashed her dark eyes at Glaxus. "Do you think Cornelius will be fed to animals in the arena?"

"Hah!" snorted Macro. "Here's a girl who knows what's right!"

"That will not be for me to decide," Glaxus told her. "Do you know where he is at the present time?"

"He spends his afternoons at a private bath in the Aventine district. He thinks the public baths are too crowded. His father and brother go with him."

"Have you heard them say anything about us or their plots against us?" asked Calvinia.

"No. My mother and I are excluded from their private talks and Cornelius would beat me if he caught me listening."

Glaxus found that easy to believe. "Once the crimes of your stepfather and stepbrothers become known to the Emperor, he may punish them by confiscating their lands and fortunes. He may also banish or execute them. What will become of you and your mother if that happens?"

"Calvinia asked me that in the baths. My real brother is a wealthy merchant in Pompeii. We'll probably live with him. Mother may be angry at me for not consulting her, but she won't be sorry to be rid of my stepfather and stepbrothers. She remarried too hastily after my father's death and she knows it."

"Then here is our plan," said Glaxus. "We'll go first to the temple of Castor and Pollux in the old forum. You'll then put the pouch under your cloak and proceed alone to the Emperor's house on the Palatine. Being a member of a senatorial family, you should be able to speak directly to Prefect Strabo. But as an additional stratagem to get you past slaves bribed by Cornelius, say you bear an important message from him. Since it's his money that's bribing them, they'll quickly let you through. Wait until you are face to face with the Prefect before making any mention of the pouch."

"I understand, but Strabo will probably want to see you personally, Centurion."

"Yes, and perhaps the rest of us as well. Tell him we'll be waiting on the temple steps and ask him to send an armed detail to fetch us directly into his presence. This will be necessary because of the slaves who lie in wait for us. Tell him I'll be standing on the steps in my uniform."

Calvinia put an arm around the girl's shoulders. "And you must eat and drink nothing while you are on the Palatine, Sylvia."

"I know. I've heard the rumors of how Empress Livia poisons those who stand between her son and his chance to succeed Augustus."

"We are not opposed to the succession of Tiberius," said Glaxus. "But the bribed slaves are planning to stop me with the same method, so avoid all food and drink. Now let's be on our way."

The late afternoon crowd in the old forum was thin. Most Romans were at the baths or at home preparing for the evening meal. Glaxus hoped to see the Athenian philosophers in their usual place, but they were gone. It was no matter. Calvinia or Pindocles could tell them later about their colleague's betrayal.

At the temple of Castor and Pollux, Glaxus checked the bindings on Trion's wrists while Macro bound his feet also. They left him sitting forlornly at the western end of the temple steps. At the eastern end, Glaxus turned Sylvia so she could see the Palatine rising above and behind the forum. She nodded and removed her cloak as he handed her the pouch. Slipping its strap over her slight shoulders, she put her cloak back on and smiled up at him. Pushing away his doubts, he patted her arm and she began walking.

Pindocles watched her vanish through the Arch of Augustus, then turned to Glaxus. "Have no fear, Centurion. Not even the god Hermes can be a better messenger for us than she. Since Cornelius would never consider trusting the future of the empire to a young girl, he could never imagine his enemies doing so. She will be completely unsuspected."

"I hope you're right." Glaxus sat wearily on the temple steps. "First an angry innkeeper and now a lovesick girl. On such pegs do the gods hang the fate of Rome."

Calvinia sat next to Glaxus. "It's nearly over. After we see Strabo, we'll all be free of this. And as for the pegs the gods use, Augustus himself may be the weakest among them. Ever since the massacre there have been rumors that he wanders about his home in a daze, leaving his hair untrimmed and face unshaven."

"So I've heard," Macro said. "And some claim that he knocks his head against walls and shouts for Varus to return his legions to him."

"Not unlikely behavior," suggested Pindocles. "He's seventy-two years old. For a man of that age to bear such great responsibility is asking much. The strain may be exacting its price."

"But Varus was his mistake!" snapped Glaxus. "So let him suffer for it!"

Pindocles responded calmly. "Would you tell him that to his face?"

Glaxus remembered how Plutarius put that same question to him just before dying. He regretted his sudden outburst, knowing his answer hadn't changed since then. "No, I wouldn't."

"Of course not," added Macro. "And if we're wise, none of us will mention it to Prefect Strabo, for it would surely reach the Emperor. That could mean our lives."

"What if it did?" Pindocles asked. "Does death not ultimately swallow all of us anyway? And does time not swallow all events? In the distant future will anyone care about the massacre in Germania? I doubt it. Nor will anyone care how each Roman lived and died, our good deeds and bad, or anything else about us."

"I don't accept that," answered Calvinia firmly. "Neither do you, Pindocles, or you wouldn't be helping us. Whatever empires are raised and ruined in ages hereafter, I cannot believe our present strivings are in vain. The choices of every Roman today will echo in the lives of unborn millions. I doubt that not for a moment." She placed one hand on Glaxus' arm and held out the other to Macro and the doctor. "Despite its faults, Rome will be forever known as this brave old world that had such people in it."

Pindocles smiled and pointed to the senate house. "You're smooth of speech and sharp of thought, Calvinia. You could be speaking in there."

She laughed. "A female senator?"

"That would never be allowed," said Glaxus.

"Not here and now," agreed the physician. "But perhaps one day the worth of a mind won't be judged by the body that carries it."

The shadows of the temple's columns had grown long when Glaxus heard the familiar tread of soldiers marching in formation. He and Calvinia stood as the first row of Praetorian Guards passed through the Arch of Augustus. At the side of the man leading them was Sylvia, nearly running to keep up.

"Strabo must have sent her along to make sure of identifying us."

"He didn't send her, Glaxus," said Calvinia. "He brought her. That tall man she's walking near is the Prefect himself."

"Ten rows of ten," observed Macro. "He not only came in person, but brought an entire century with him. There's no doubt he's taking this matter seriously."

Pindocles had silently glided up the temple steps to stand beside Glaxus. "Whatever happens, you must not lose yourself as you did with Trion. Trust that the truth, calmly and clearly spoken, will prevail."

"Calmly and clearly," repeated Glaxus, then took a deep breath before walking down the steps.

Strabo halted his troops before the temple. He was a formidable sight. Equal in stature to Glaxus, he wore a glistening helmet with breastplate to match. Glaxus noticed scars on his forearms. Apparently, he'd actually served as a soldier at one time and was not merely a politician in armor as Varus had been.

The Prefect bent over and whispered to Sylvia. The girl nodded, pointing first at Glaxus, then at each of the others. Strabo fixed his steely eyes on them one by one. When he spoke, Glaxus recognized the tone of a man who was accustomed to being obeyed.

"You are Senior Centurion Glaxus of the 19th Legion?"

"Yes sir."

"A survivor of the disaster in Germania?"

"Yes sir."

"I am Seius Strabo, Prefect of the Praetorian Guard. I have read the tablets which you brought and have passed them on to the Emperor. Because of the information in them, he wishes to see you and your party immediately. Tribune Cornelius has also been summoned."

Glaxus' heart began to race. He had expected an interrogation by Strabo, but the Emperor must have considered the matter too important to delegate. He could see on his comrades' faces that they shared his alarm, yet they certainly knew there was only one reply he could make.

"Yes sir."

Sylvia was sent home with an escort of four Praetorians. Two others cut the bindings on Trion's feet and took him to the rear of the formation. Glaxus and Calvinia walked at the front on Strabo's right with Pindocles and Macro on the left.

As they went through the arch toward the Palatine, Glaxus moved nearer to Calvinia. "You must help me. What should I know before we arrive?"

She kept her voice as low as his. "Although everyone refers to Augustus as the Emperor, he prefers to be addressed as Princeps, the First Citizen of Rome. Under normal circumstances he's courteous, polite, and reasonably tolerant of criticism. However, if the rumors are true, his conduct may be very different now because of his anguish over the massacre."

"Then we must be cautious. When were you last in his presence?"

"A year before he ordered my father's removal from the senate for taking bribes."

"How do you think he'll react when he sees you again?"

"I truly don't know. In his current state of mind, he may not even remember me." Calvinia frowned. "Perhaps it would be better if he didn't."

Glaxus couldn't agree. "I think the more clearly Augustus recalls you, the more it will strengthen our position. When he sees that the daughter of a disgraced senator has risked her life to reveal an enemy of the empire, how can he not take our side?"

"He'll admire me for my dedication to Rome regardless of what happened to my father?"

"Exactly."

"Or perhaps he'll think me an opportunist whose trying to get him to re-establish my family honor and fortune. He might then become disgusted with the whole business and simply order execution for everyone involved. You, me, Cornelius, the whole lot of us. Don't forget that when he was young and ascending to power, he participated eagerly in the great proscription."

"Yes, I know." It was before Glaxus was born, but his parents had often mentioned it. Rome was in turmoil after Julius Caesar's assassination. The struggle for political control ended temporarily when Augustus, known then as Octavian, formed the Second Triumvirate with Marc Antony and Aemilius Lepidus. Prominent men who opposed this arrangement were shown no mercy. Their funds and property were seized, then the legions were commanded to slaughter them and their families. Roman troops murdered Roman citizens by the thousands. Not even Cicero was spared. Glaxus' father once spoke of seeing the great orator's head and hands placed on display in the forum.

Augustus was undoubtedly ruthless in the past, though that was long ago. In the years since, he'd earned a reputation for discernment and tolerance, as Calvinia had said. But with the possibility of a Germanic invasion hanging over the city, would he simply lash out indiscriminately at any threat to his authority? Would he not bother to weed out the bad from the good, choosing instead to have everyone involved instantly killed? Calvinia might be right about that also. It would certainly be the easiest solution. The Emperor was already threatening men with execution for not joining the emergency army units.

Glaxus struggled to clear his mind. Such speculation was useless. The answers would come soon enough. Once through the arch, they turned right past the residence of the Vestal Virgins and left onto the Via Nova. Above and to the south, he saw the Great Mother's huge temple looming against the sky. Out of sight just behind it was Augustus' home.

XIII

The Emperor's house was as simple as Glaxus was always told. Not small, but certainly not imposing, it sat on the eastern end of the Palatine hill overlooking the Circus Maximus. All Rome knew it once belonged to Senator Hortensius, one of those killed in the great proscription. Even so, Augustus expressed no qualms about confiscating it and had lived there ever since. Glaxus heard about it being partially destroyed by fire six years ago and rebuilt in the same modest style. Its colonnades were short and made of local stone rather than expensive imported material. Any mansion on the Campus Agrippae was larger and more elegant, but the Emperor was famous for not engaging in ostentatious display. He also discouraged extravagance among his family. His daughter Julia once built a lavish residence which he promptly had demolished.

Strabo ordered most of the century to wait on the Via Nova while he and ten men took Glaxus and the others up to the house. Once through the outer door and in the vestibule, he left them to wait with the Praetorians. The three male slaves on duty in the vestibule nervously avoided eye contact with the soldiers.

Glaxus wondered if these slaves were among those Cornelius had bribed to poison him. One of them kept glancing at a table on which there was a jug of wine and several goblets. Sylvia had certainly spoken of the bribing to Strabo who had just as surely mentioned it to Augustus. There would likely be a complete purging of the Emperor's houschold slaves in which even the innocent might perish. Glaxus would bear no blame for this, but regretted it nonetheless.

When Strabo returned, he ordered Glaxus and the others to remove all weapons. Pindocles did so last, making a show of removing the bejeweled dagger from its hiding place. The Prefect watched with a grin, but still wanted to examine the other sleeve. He then led them through the inner door into the atrium. Eight soldiers were told to stay in the vestibule while two others hauled in the plainly terrified Trion.

Glaxus removed his helmet and glanced around. The house was simple inside as well as out. Oil lamps hanging from the ceiling revealed no mosaics on the floors or marble statues for decoration, though there were some frescoes on the walls. Strabo escorted them across the atrium and into the tablinum, the reception room where they would likely wait for Augustus. It was already occupied by at least a dozen men crowding around a large table. These were obviously assistants of various sorts and were chattering back and forth in loud tones, even shouting at times.

Glaxus guessed such clamoring would stop when Augustus entered, but then he was surprised to hear the Prefect say, "I have brought them, Princeps."

"The Centurion first, Strabo. The others can keep their distance for the moment."

"Yes, Princeps. Come forward, Centurion."

The Emperor was dressed in such a simple style and surrounded by so many aides, Glaxus hadn't realized he was in the room. The aides finally fell silent as they receded from the table, revealing him sitting behind heaps of maps, scrolls, and tablets. Those that Glaxus had brought were lying directly before him. A dice board was on a stool nearby.

After a lifetime of hearing about Augustus, Glaxus was now in front of the man and resolved to take a close look. While every bit of seventy-two years old, the Emperor had retained a handsome face despite eyebrows that met over a curving nose. His teeth were few and widely spaced. True to the rumors, he was unshaven and his untrimmed hair curled over his smallish ears. His gray locks still bore traces of youthful blondeness. A row of bruises stood out on his forehead, as though he had indeed beaten it against a wall. As Glaxus approached, the Emperor slowly stood up. He wore thick-soled sandals to make himself seem tall. Without them, Glaxus guessed him to be no more than five and a half feet. He was also wearing several tunics, presumably to fend off the November cold. His voice was not deep.

"You brought these tablets from Tribune Lucius?"

"Yes, Princeps." Glaxus pounded his fist on his chest and saluted. "Senior Centurion Glaxus Claudius Valtinius of the 19th Legion at Fort Vetera."

"Yes, yes, you needn't be so formal. I've read everything you brought. I always knew Cornelius and his clan were ambitious, but this is still a surprise. The girl Sylvia told Strabo that gladiators owned by the Tribune's father mounted an attack against you last night." The Emperor pointed at Trion. "And she said they were led by that whimpering wretch."

"Yes, Princeps. They attacked us at an inn on the Via Flaminia."

"Such scheming requires a strong response, but we will lay that aside until the Tribune is here. He has been sent for, Strabo?"

"Yes sir. His father and brother have been ordered to come as well."

"Inform me upon their arrival." Augustus returned his gaze to Glaxus. "The situation when you left Germania was desperate?"

"Yes sir. Tribune Lucius was preparing to evacuate Fort Aliso and retreat west across the Rhine to Fort Vetera. Tribune Asprenas was bringing two legions north from the Main River in an attempt to halt the Gauls at the Rhine. Tribune Lucius put this information and more in the tablets he sent with me, sir."

"That he did, and with much candor. Further dispatches from Lucius were delivered this morning telling me that he and Asprenas have succeeded. Aliso was safely evacuated and the Gauls chose to halt at the Rhine when they found themselves facing the two legions. They quickly withdrew to the northeast and there are signs that Herman's affiliation of tribes is already disintegrating. I have also ordered Tiberius back to Germania."

Glaxus was glad to hear that Lucius saved the people under his command and had been instrumental in halting the Gauls. That would make it hard for the Emperor to resent his being so bluntly honest in the tablets.

"Unfortunately, the standards you buried were discovered by the Gauls. Lucius saw them being brandished by the tribesmen who advanced on Aliso." The Emperor waved forward an aide who placed a jug on the table. "And something else arrived today. Show him."

The aide reached into the jug and pulled out the rotting, but still recognizable head of Varus, dripping with cedar oil.

"Herman sent it to Marobodus in the hopes of persuading him to join the rebellion, as you told Lucius in the tablets. Marobodus refused to join and sent it on to me." The Emperor waved his hand again and the aide returned the head to the jug. "Lucius writes very frankly of the General's arrogance and incompetence. I also see those faults in Varus' written reply to you." As the Emperor gently fingered his bruised forehead, anguish and regret were evident on his face. "Centurion, do you believe I made an error in judgment by putting Varus in command?"

Glaxus opened his mouth, but swiftly closed it. He had told Plutarius and Pindocles that he would never confront the Emperor with the folly of giving command to Varus. Yet now the question had been directly asked and the opportunity presented. He swallowed hard and opened his mouth again.

"Yes sir. You were wrong to make Varus supreme commander of the Germanic legions. It was equally foolish to trust Herman and a bad policy to attempt colonization beyond the Rhine. The entire enterprise was unwise. These are my honest opinions, Princeps."

With the Emperor's eyes lingering on him, Glaxus began to feel unwise himself.

Augustus held up the tablet containing the replies of Varus and Cornelius. "That's why you saved this? To present as evidence in case Varus' inadequacy led to disaster?"

"Yes sir."

"It bears sword cuts and is stained with your blood."

"Yes sir. It was beneath my armor when the massacre began."

"So I read. Your courage was well noted by Lucius in his description of your wounds." Augustus reached out to touch the emblem of the 19th Legion on Glaxus' chest. "You must believe that your suffering and sacrifice had purpose, Centurion, and that your comrades did not die in vain. Even from this catastrophe lessons can be learned. I will advise Tiberius that upon replacing me, he should seek to stabilize the empire's borders and not expand them."

The Emperor paused to open the tablet. "It's well known that years ago I used a document written by Marc Antony as a weapon against him. I seized his will from the temple of Vesta and read it to the senate. It revealed his treasonous conspiracy with Cleopatra to rule the empire from Egypt. His own words in his own hand helped to bring about his defeat. Cornelius shall fall in the same way."

"May I suggest, Princeps, that we let the Centurion and the others wait out of sight while the Tribune is brought in with his father and brother. Then you may reveal what you know whenever you wish."

"Well thought of, Strabo. We'll do so. For that young toad to think he could succeed me is ridiculous!"

"If I may speak, Princeps." Calvinia's voice rose firmly from the far side of the tablinum. "His intent now is to succeed Tiberius."

Augustus stepped from behind the table and squinted in Calvinia's direction. Taking Glaxus' arm, he crossed the room with a slight limp in his left leg. "She sounds familiar. Tell me her name."

"Calvinia, Princeps. She is my betrothed and the daughter of Senator Valerius Andorus."

"Ah, yes." The Emperor wrapped his hands around hers. "I remember you well. Your father was corrupt, so I expelled him from the senate and confiscated his personal fortune. He became ill and died not long after, true?"

Glaxus watched Calvinia's face and could tell she wanted to withdraw her hands.

But she didn't. "Yes, Princeps. Very true."

The Emperor peered into her eyes. "And you resent me for it."

"There was no doubt of my father's corruption."

"None, and I dealt with him as I dealt with others guilty of the same offense."

"You knew Varus was thoroughly corrupt," she said. "You knew it when he was consul and also when he was governor of Syria. Yet you gave him your niece in marriage and put him in command of the Germanic legions."

Glaxus gritted his teeth. A glance to his right told him Macro was doing the same. Only Pindocles smiled.

"I admit that was a grievous mistake, Calvinia. I'm an old man and old men often value friendship more than they should. Varus had been my friend for years, perhaps so long that I became blind to his misdeeds and shortcomings. But that doesn't excuse your father."

"I ask for no posthumous pardon, Princeps. My father's death was a relief. It enabled me to break an engagement to Senator Hyboreas."

"And you will instead marry Centurion Glaxus?"

"Yes."

"Then I ask that you begin your new life with no bitterness, either toward me or your father's memory." Augustus leaned closer to her. "You think I haven't discovered that you've been reduced to running a butcher shop in the Emporium?"

Calvinia stared at him. "How?"

"You borrowed the money for the shop from your aunt. She told one of her slaves who told one of Strabo's who promptly told him. Strabo then told me. There is little that goes on among the families of senators and equites that does not reach me eventually." He gently touched her head wound. "The gladiators did this to you last night?"

"Yes, Princeps."

"Such valor should not go unrecognized." Augustus turned to Glaxus. "Centurion, do you possess a personal fortune of at least 400,000 sestertii?"

Glaxus recalled this was the minimum amount a man must have to be made a member of the equites, Rome's second level of nobility just below the senators. He had saved up slightly more than that during his time in the army. "Yes sir. It's in a bank here in Rome, but I—"

"Then you will be the wife of an eques," the Emperor told Calvinia, "and a member of the nobility once again. This will be in addition to the pension and farmland he is entitled to as a retired veteran. Is that satisfactory?"

When Calvinia looked at Glaxus, he shook his head. She then smiled at the Emperor. "Thank you, Princeps, but my future husband wants only what he is legally entitled to."

"You will let me do nothing for you?"

"Yes, Princeps," said Glaxus. "There is a child mentioned in the tablets whom we wish to make our own. She's the daughter of an auxiliary who died in the massacre. Because she's Germanic, there might be hostility toward our adopting her."

"Ah, Yes. Hilda. The adoption formalities will go smoothly. I will see to it." The Emperor now stepped in front of Trion. "Your name!"

The trembling Greek flapped his lips in vain, so the Emperor looked at Glaxus.

"His name is Trion, sir. He's a teacher of rhetoric."

"Why did you lead the gladiators sent by Cornelius? Answer me!"

"Mercy, Princeps! Mercy!"

"I will show you the same mercy you would have shown the Centurion and his friends, unless you speak honestly about your part in this."

Trion had to be held up by the two Praetorians as the words came spilling out of him. "I already knew something of the Tribune's plot against the Centurion. I was in the forum with the other Greek teachers when he came to us for help. I learned of the tablets he carried and also of the one being brought by Pindocles."

"You then went to Cornelius' home to reveal what you had discovered?"

"Yes, Princeps. The Tribune, along with his father and brother, promised me position and money if I led their assassins to recover the tablets. After killing the Centurion and his companions, we were to go to Ancona to find and kill the doctor and recover that tablet also." Trion finished, then stared pleadingly at the Emperor.

"Truthfully spoken," Augustus declared. "You have earned clemency. Instead of giving you to beasts in the arena, I will allow you to drink poison. Take him into one of the side chambers until I call for him again."

Trion turned pale as the Praetorians dragged him away.

The Emperor next aimed his gaze at Pindocles. "You are the physician everyone was trying to find? The one whose letter of warning to the Centurion informed him you had the incriminating tablet?"

"Yes, Princeps. I am Pindocles, formerly assigned to the 19th Legion."

Augustus spoke over his shoulder to Strabo. "Another cunning Greek who selected what he guessed would be the winning side, only this one guessed rightly. The question now is what reward he expects of me." The Emperor pushed his fist against Pindocles' chest. "The wisest thing my Roman ancestors ever did was conquer your country!"

As Pindocles raised an eyebrow, it was clear a nerve had been struck. Glaxus only hoped the physician wouldn't behead himself.

"There are many ways to conquer, Princeps. My gods have become your gods under different names. Also, the fluid Greek language gradually wins its victory over your inflexible Latin throughout the empire. Far into the future my tongue shall remain in use when yours has been discarded. Who will have conquered then? As for rewards, I want none. I am resigning from the army medical service so I may return to Athens to teach the healing arts."

For the first time since the audience began, the Emperor laughed. "You speak your mind without fear, as Greek a trait as ever there was. Your service to Rome is not unappreciated, but if no reward is what you want, that is what I gladly give you. Good journey to Athens. Now tell me, Centurion, who is this companion of yours with the unyoked eyes? His right one looks at me while his left watches the ceiling."

"Sir, this is Macro Fulvianus, an optio of mine in the 19th."

"A survivor of the massacre?"

"No sir. He lost his eye in a bear hunt on which we were sent. He was then discharged before the campaign began. His friendship and courage in this matter have been invaluable."

"What is your occupation now, citizen?"

Macro hastily straightened his glass eye. "I'm a merchant in Ostia, Princeps."

"Your business flourishes?"

"Yes sir, it does."

"Then you too would like to forgo a reward?"

"Actually, Princeps, if there's an opening in the Praetorian Guard—"

"There is not. Thank you for your service to your country." The Emperor turned away and limped back to the table. "Speaking of bears, I recently received three magnificent specimens from Germania. They're still in holding pens at the Taurus Amphitheatre. They were meant for the gladiator games I postponed after hearing of the massacre. Did you capture them, Centurion?"

"No, Princeps. Our attempt failed. Your bears were captured under the command of Tribune Cornelius."

"Ah, yes. I remember him bragging to me about it." A cold grin stole across the Emperor's face. "What an ironic possibility that brings to mind." He noticed an approaching aide. "The Tribune has arrived?"

"Yes, Princeps. He waits in the vestibule with his father and brother."

"Bring them before me." Augustus sat at the table and spoke to Strabo. "Take our four friends into the same room with the Greek traitor. Bring out the Centurion when I use my old saying about asparagus. You won't have to wait long."

"Yes sir."

Strabo entered last, then left the door open a crack so Glaxus could observe. Tydus strode swiftly into the tablinum with Cornelius and Falco on either side of him. All three wore white togas, Tydus' bearing the purple trim of his senatorial rank.

Cornelius had gotten his hair curled, but otherwise appeared no different from when Glaxus last saw him at Fort Aliso. That expression of disdain was still on his face. This imperial summons apparently didn't worry him. Falco seemed less confident. He swayed slightly from side to side, his small eyes blinking rapidly as he looked over at Cornelius. Their father was a man of about fifty. His loud, smooth voice seemed to leap out of him, probably from many years of practice in the senate.

"Hail, Princeps! My sons and I came as soon as your order reached us. How may we serve you?"

"By falling on your swords quicker than cooked asparagus. Perhaps Centurion Glaxus will volunteer to hold the Tribune's."

As he saw Cornelius' face stiffen with fear, Glaxus felt Strabo tap him on the shoulder. "Now, Centurion. You and the woman come with me."

Glaxus watched his three foes stare as he walked through the door between Calvinia and the Prefect.

"But Princeps!" shouted Cornelius. "This man was long an opponent of mine in the 19th Legion! His lies are—"

"Bluster will not save you, Tribune! You betrayed your comrades to the enemy and lied to me about your courage at the massacre. I have the testimony of Centurion Glaxus and of your fellow Tribunes Lucius and Decimus. The Centurion brought it to me on tablets this very hour. In them he describes a conversation he had with you at Fort Aliso in which you told him you plan to hold my position one day. You also attempted to kill him and his friends by employing your gladiators and bribing my slaves. Your brother and father knew of your betrayal and deception and joined you in your plotting. How do you answer all this? I suggest you speak the entire truth while you have the chance."

Glaxus exchanged whispers with Strabo. "Prefect, the Emperor didn't tell him Pindocles got through with the most incriminating tablet."

"The Emperor offers the Tribune an opportunity to save himself with honesty. Let us see if he makes use of it."

Cornelius recovered somewhat and addressed Augustus calmly. "As I began to say, Princeps, the Centurion is a lying plebeian who envies my rank and abilities. I would never seek to occupy your place. The gods alone bestow that on whom they choose. He must have created these wild tales of gladiators and bribing to destroy your opinion of me and to gain your favor. Concerning the testimony of my fellow tribunes, Lucius was not at the massacre and my friend Decimus lost his life in it. This all amounts to nothing, Princeps. Anyone can write anything on a tablet."

"Fool!" hissed Strabo.

Glaxus realized that Cornelius knew nothing about the status of his assassins. Though they obviously failed to kill Glaxus, he was gambling they had succeeded with Pindocles.

"Yes, Tribune." The Emperor patted the stack of tablets on the table. "Anyone can write anything on one of these." He held up the bloodstained tablet and opened it to display Cornelius' family seal. "As you did here."

Glaxus saw Cornelius tightly shut his eyes, as though in pain. He had wagered and lost.

Strabo now gestured to the two soldiers to bring in Trion, then Pindocles and Macro followed. Senator Tydus seemed at the edge of panic when he saw Trion, but fought hard for control before speaking to Augustus.

"I urged my sons against this course of action, Princeps, but they wouldn't listen."

"Liar!" yelped Falco. "You agreed with Cornelius to hire the gladiators!"

"Silence!" The Emperor slammed the tablet onto the table. "The testimony of your worthless accomplice Trion together with the Tribune's own written words has finished the three of you. Your cowardice, treason, and murderous ambition must be punished. All lands, property, and personal fortunes you possess will be confiscated. As for your lives..."

Cornelius' hands shook as he held them out to the Emperor. "Please, Princeps! I beg for banishment and not death!"

"You plead only for yourself?"

"You may do as you wish with my father and brother!"

"I may do as I wish with you all."

"Cornelius brought this upon us!" cried Falco. "Banish us, Princeps, and let him die!"

Augustus turned in his chair and spoke to Glaxus. "They have wronged you more than anyone, Centurion. How would you decide if you sat where I sit? Banishment or death?"

Glaxus couldn't help asking himself what these three would learn if allowed to live. He glanced at Calvinia. What did she want him to do? How broadly would she draw the line between mercy and justice? As she gazed calmly at the floor, she seemed to be leaving the choice to him.

He stepped forward. "It's not I they have most wronged, Princeps. It's their fellow Romans who died in the massacre. If I sat where you sit, I would order them to do as you already have. Fall upon their swords." After Glaxus said this, he noticed that Calvinia kept her face down and completely neutral.

Cornelius went limp while Tydus appeared grim and resigned. Falco improbably tried to run, only to be seized by Strabo.

"That's still too good for them!" barked Augustus. "In the old days traitors were hurled to their doom from atop the Tarpeian Rock. Or I could have the Tribune fed to his own bears. What say you, Centurion?"

Calvinia now looked up at Glaxus and frowned.

He nodded at her. If the line between mercy and justice was broad, then the line dividing justice from vengeance would need to be even broader. "I think what has to be done is best done quickly, Princeps, and with no enjoyment. I also ask that they be allowed to say farewell to their family and be given proper cremation and funeral rites."

"It is so ordered. Have them escorted home by the Praetorians, Strabo. If they cannot find it in themselves to die by their own hands, the soldiers are to help them. Remove the Greek traitor as well and get some poison into him."

"Yes sir."

As Cornelius was taken out, he turned toward Glaxus with a blank stare. Glaxus guessed he would need the Praetorians' help.

"We'll have to replace all the second-level slaves in both my residence and yours, Strabo. We have no way of knowing which were bribed."

"Yes, Princeps. Do you want them to die also?"

The Emperor drummed his fingers on the table, peering at Glaxus, at Calvinia, and finally at the Prefect again.

"No. We've had enough death for today. Give them three lashes each and reassign them to my farms." Augustus sighed and rubbed his hands over his face. "I'm an old dog who's lived too long. I've seen the treachery of Caesar's killers, the arrogance of Antony, and now the plotting of Cornelius. In future times, men may reshape the world, but what fills their hearts today will fill them always. Greed, ambition, and lust for power shall outlast the stars." He waved Glaxus forward. "Come here, Centurion."

When Glaxus walked over to the table, the Emperor reached across it and grasped him firmly by the forearms. "Once again I thank you and your friends most deeply for your dedication and service to Rome. You must never regret that service."

"I will not, Princeps."

"Good." Augustus pointed toward the vestibule. "Now get out of my sight."

XIV

When they were in the vestibule preparing to leave, Strabo insisted that the four of them dine with him and stay the night at his house on the Esquiline. The next morning, he told Glaxus to come see him in seven days. "I will have ready your diploma of military retirement, the first payment of your pension, and the deed to your farmland. If you're prepared to adopt the child Hilda, I will remind the Emperor about smoothing out the formalities."

"Thank you, sir. Calvinia and I will be married in Ostia in the coming week. When we return to Rome to see you, we'll close her shop and repay her aunt. Hilda will be with us. Could the adoption process be completed by that time?"

"Yes. I'll be sure it's been settled and the child will be yours. Then what? To your farmland?"

"Yes sir."

"Even though colonization east of the Rhine will not be attempted again, Tiberius will still be leading a punitive force into that region to find Herman. Are you sure you don't want to go along as Chief Centurion? I had your service record brought to me last night after everyone else went to bed. You're eminently qualified."

"Thank you, Prefect, but I believe I have done all that duty demands."

"No one would argue with that. Good luck to you then, and enjoy civilian life."

On the street outside Strabo's house, Glaxus put a hand on Pindocles' shoulder. "Good-bye, Greek. Thank you and safe journey to Athens."

"Couldn't you delay your trip and come to our wedding?" Calvinia asked.

"I'll be master of ceremonies," said Macro. "It will be quite a celebration."

Pindocles smiled and shook his head. "I would only be out of place. I'll visit my countrymen here for a day, then travel south on the Via Appia to Brundisium to find a ship bound for Greece. May the gods grant you joy and favor as you begin your life together." He turned and padded down the street, his black robes billowing about him in the morning breeze.

Glaxus watched the physician go and wished him nothing but good. Though he could be arrogant, there was a cold integrity about him that had been refreshing to deal with.

They were on a barge to Ostia an hour later. When they arrived at Macro's insula, Hilda threw herself at Glaxus.

"Pater meus! Is all well?"

"All is well. Hilda, this is Calvinia. She will be my mater familias."

"Then I'll call her mater meus." Hilda took Calvinia's hand. "You're beautiful, my mother."

"As your real mother must have been to have so lovely a daughter." Calvinia stroked the girl's blonde hair. "You must tell me all you remember of your parents, Hilda. You must also set your memories down in tablets so you'll have them close to you as you grow older. Can you read and write Latin as well as speak it?"

"No."

"Then you must learn. In the meantime, I'll write them down for you."

"Can we begin tomorrow?"

"We'll begin tonight after dinner. Tomorrow and the next few days will be very busy."

Glaxus watched them standing hand in hand as they talked and felt himself to be quite fortunate.

Dinner that evening was long and loud. Macro's entire family joined in wishing prosperity to Calvinia and Glaxus. Afterwards,

Calvinia took Hilda to a corner of the dining room and sat with her beneath an oil lamp to start writing. The night was growing cold, so Glaxus and Macro began closing the windows. Reaching out for a shutter, Glaxus noticed the stars of Orion the Hunter rising in the eastern sky. He paused a moment to watch them shine.

The Emperor said greed, ambition, and lust for power would outlast the stars and always fill the hearts of men. Glaxus didn't doubt that, yet he was convinced honor and forbearance were just as eternal. He'd seen such qualities of goodness in Germania and in Rome. Even Augustus showed a spark of them. As long as there were people in the world, Glaxus was certain the ancient battle between virtue and sin would be waged in every soul. He was equally certain that virtue would be victorious more often than not. While the Athenian philosophers might say that was too simple, he knew it was so.

It had to be.

Closing the shutter, he went to sit with Calvinia and Hilda.

Printed in the United States
44306LVS00002BA/22-33